CW00493144

Game Plan

This is a work of fiction. Names, characters, places, and incidents either are the products of the author's imagination or are used fictitiously. Any resemblance to actual persons, living or dead, businesses, companies, events, or locales is entirely coincidental.

CHAPTER ONE

Connor

*E*veryone had a soulmark - a name, written somewhere on their body, that usually showed up before they'd even finished elementary school. It was the name of a soulmate, the one person in the world who was most perfectly and totally compatible. Academics studied it, funded research into couples who'd found theirs, or people who hadn't. There was still no definitive answer as to how it worked, or why the marks showed up in different places and at different times.

Connor's had appeared overnight, a week before his tenth birthday, and mostly Connor remembered being *annoyed*. His dad had promised a pool party, and Connor didn't want to have to wear a t-shirt to go swimming. His mom had taken him to the mall, getting him a pack of stickers to wear over the 'Ashley' that curved around his upper arm.

The stickers weren't perfect. They covered your soulmark, and they were specially adapted to hold on through any kind of activity, but they didn't really look like *skin*. It was rude to point it out, and even ruder to ask someone their soulmark's name. Of course, ten-year-olds don't care much about being rude, so Connor had been asked a lot.

3

Connor was *still* asked a lot. It was one of the (very few) downsides of being Connor Lewis, up-and-coming star of the Madison Howlers. Press and fans were always asking, no matter how many times Connor brushed them off. He didn't really *get* everyone's fascination. It was just a name, and there was no guarantee that Connor would ever meet the 'right' Ashley. (There had been *three* Ashleys in Connor's high school class, and Connor hadn't liked even one of them.)

"Over here! Connor!" the crowd was calling for him, someone waving a microphone in Connor's face. "How does it feel to have scored the winning goal?" He grinned, pleased to have his feat recognized.

"It feels great," he answered, catching a look from Hayden Nickson. *He* was probably being asked what it had felt like *not* to score the winning goal. Hayden was older, had been playing with the Howlers longer, and Connor looked up to him a lot. He seemed to have a knack for getting the press off his ass, which Connor could really have used.

Despite playing for a few years now, Connor still wasn't used to the attention. He loved hockey and talking about hockey, but the press somehow seemed to put him on edge. Connor wished he didn't feel so stupid, giving the same answers all the time.

"Connor!" A different journalist waved Connor over, pushing a stunning girl in a 'Heart the Howlers' t-shirt in Connor's general direction. "Connor, this is Laila Briggs. She's a fan." She smiled, and somehow she looked even more beautiful. It caught Connor off-guard, and he beamed back, lifting a hand to rub across the back of his neck.

"It's so great to meet you, Connor," Laila was gushing, fingers toying with the hem of her shirt. "I've wanted to, ever since you were signed. You see -" She lifted the fabric, just enough to reveal a line of script – black letters spelling out CONNOR. Before Connor could even wonder if it was real, or just a convincing tattoo, Laila giggled. "I think you *must* be my soulmate. Can I -" Her other hand came up, her nails running across Connor's arm as she went for the sticker that covered his soulmark.

Connor snatched his arm away and was proud of himself for telling neither Laila nor the reporter to fuck off.

"That's not on, and you know it," he growled, clamping his fingers at his sides to resist the urge to check the security of the sticker. It would only draw attention to it. What Connor needed was to get away from the crowd and sort himself out.

He only did so slowly, answering the same question three more times, giving less and less enthusiastic answers. Finally, he pushed the locker room door shut behind him and leaned against it with a heavy sigh.

"Everything alright?" Hayden asked, and Connor gave a deep laugh.

"Fucking hell, Nix, I didn't even *see* you there."

"Should've looked, then, shouldn't you?" Hayden asked, and Connor had to admit he had a point. Hayden was standing at his locker, making no attempt to hide himself.

"How do you keep so cool, out there?" Connor asked, moving slowly to start stripping out of his uniform.

"On the ice, or with the press?" Hayden asked back. Connor gave him a look and was gratified when Hayden laughed. "It's just practice," he said. "It helps to be boring. They can only write so many articles about how Hayden Nickson is not looking for a soulmate at this time before they get tired of it."

Wrapping a towel around his hips, Hayden glanced around, like he was about to impart some great secret. "Or you can do what James does, take a different girl home every week." That made Connor laugh, and he felt as if a weight had lifted slightly off his shoulders. It still sucked, to constantly be asked questions on a topic he didn't give a damn about, but the camaraderie and the success of the Madison Howlers were worth the sacrifice.

When Connor got outside, showered and dressed, there were only a few members of staff still hanging around. They were mostly swapping cigarettes before their drive home. Though he felt better after his shower, he still slowed when a cigarette was held out to him by Tex Banks, head of rink security. "You deserve it, after a goal like that," he offered. Connor grinned, lifting the cigarette to his lips to take a drag.

"I told you, I quit," he teased, make Tex rumble with laughter.

"Sure, sure, and you don't tell Jeannie that you get them from me." It was his and Tex's secret agreement. Tex shared his cigarettes, Connor didn't tell Tex's wife he hadn't kicked the habit. It worked well.

"Connor." The soft, almost shy voice caught him by surprise. Connor was pretty sure his mouth dropped open for a moment when he spotted Laila walking across the parking lot towards him. He took a step back, and she froze. "I just - I wanted to say I'm sorry," she offered, her hair falling forward over her face.

"That guy heard me telling my friend that my soulmarks says Connor, and he said he could get me to meet you, and I thought -" She looked so hopeful.

"It's not Laila," he told her, perhaps *because* this time she hadn't even started to ask. He could see her face fall, and once again Connor simply didn't get it. Why pin so many hopes on a person you might never even meet? "Connor's a pretty common name," he offered. Though Laila smiled, Connor could tell she was faking it.

"I hope you meet her soon," Laila muttered, turning back towards the cars. Connor hoped she was going to find her ride home.

"Do I want to ask what that was all about?" Tex asked as Connor took another long drag from the cigarette. Connor shook his head. His gaze dropped to where the end of the word 'Jeannie' peeked out from under Tex's collar. It was the highest placement on the body of any soulmark he'd ever seen, though no one knew why they tended to fall below the shoulder.

"Don't worry about it," Connor advised.

◆ ◆ ◆

The *Madison Gazette* printed a story about Connor turning down a chance to meet his soulmate. At least they didn't mention Laila's name. Scott Dillon, the team's PR, clipped the piece from the sports pages and pinned it to the notice board in Coach's office. There, Connor's name joined two dozen others who'd had precisely similar stories written about them. *No* NHL player, not even the newest recruit, could meet with *every* fan who claimed a soulmate connection.

After the next day, nobody even mentioned it. They all just got their heads down, preparing for their next game. It promised to be a good one, and Connor practiced hard to make sure his passes were on point.

The Friday of the match was crisp and cool. The ice felt perfect under Connor's blades as he skated out to a roar of applause from the stands. As far as Connor could tell, they didn't stop applauding until the final whistle, at which point they went *wild*.

It had been a good game: fast, aggressive. Connor had been slammed into the wall *twice*, and he was going to have bruises all down his arm by morning. It was worth it for a second consecutive win this early in the season.

The team piled off the ice, shoving and shouting, practically drowning out the questions of the reporters who tried to gather around them.

"Calm down, calm down," came the foghorn voice of Hugo Nilsson, team Captain, making everyone else quieten down at least a *little*. "Drinks are on me!" Nilssy shouted, and the uproar started all over again.

A guy Connor recognized as a reporter for the *Wisconsin*

Tribune managed to squeeze to the bench where Connor was untying his skates.

"Can I get a picture?" he asked, gesturing past James, presumably to where a photographer was waiting. "You've had two good games. I think I can talk my editor into a sidebar - all about the rising new star." The flattery made Connor duck his head. He never knew how to respond without seeming arrogant.

"Let me shower first?" he suggested.

"If you think it will help," Blake quipped from the other side of the bench. Connor gave him a shove that sent him sprawling, smacking hard against the row of lockers. When Blake came up theatrically howling, rubbing his arm as if he wasn't still wearing elbow pads, everyone laughed. Connor slipped through them to the adjoining showers.

Prodding at his sore arm, Connor noticed that the edge of the sticker covering his soulmark had come loose. The special adhesives they used in the athletic-grade ones held up pretty well, but you needed to change them at least a couple of times a week. Secure in the knowledge that no one could make any real detail through the steam of the shower, Connor peeled it off. He had spares in his bag, he could slap a new one on before they went out for the night.

Showered and rubbed dry, Connor slung one towel casually over his shoulder, then wrapped another around his hips. Then, he joined the rest of the team, all in various states of undress.

Leaning over, Angus tapped Connor's hip. "What did you think of Charlotte Checkers' new defenseman?" he asked. Connor's answer launched them into a discussion on the dangers of an opponent who seemed equally comfortable with both offense and defense.

By the time Connor was dressed, the conversation had circled back to self-congratulation.

"Come on, Lewis," the reporter from before complained. "I've got to drive home tonight, you know."

"Like you weren't enjoying the conversation as much as

anyone," Connor retorted. There was a reason none of the reporters had left, even after most of them had got their quotes. They liked a good post-match analysis as much as the players. Connor checked his hair in the mirror, then swung his locker shut with a smirk. "Where do you want me?"

He allowed himself to be positioned, sitting with his back against the bench, looking, apparently, tired but confident. The reporter waved a hand at the rest of the team, encouraging them to mill about, for 'background-color', whatever that might be.

Other photographers had gathered too, holding their cameras up to get the best angle. Connor was grinning up at them all, ignoring Blake at a locker behind him, until he heard a snigger, and looked up -

Just in time to get the cascade of water right in the face. Surging to his feet, Connor spluttered, his clean white t-shirt drenched through, sticking to his skin.

"You asshole!" he shouted, but he was laughing, trying to brush the water off him and failing.

"You deserved it," Blake pointed out, rubbing his hand through Connor's wet hair.

The flashes of cameras were still going off, and Connor groaned, tugging his t-shirt off over his head.

It wasn't until Hayden stepped forward, putting himself between Connor's right arm and the photographers, that Connor remembered he wasn't wearing a sticker over his soulmark.

"None of you are going to publish any pictures of Connor's soulmark," Hayden said. His tone wasn't angry, but it was firm enough to command attention. Someone put a hand on Connor's back, handing him a spare shirt, which he pulled on with shaking fingers.

In fourteen years, no one had ever seen Connor's soulmark, except his mom. Knowing that the information was out there, even only among the Howlers and their trusted photographers, was disorientating. It felt like something private had been pulled away from him, leaving a *hurt* that Connor had never experienced before.

He took a deep breath, paying attention to the way his ribs moved, trying to ground himself in the physical sensation. There wasn't any reason to panic. As much as Connor trusted the Howlers, he couldn't help but picture a parade of Ashleys, all friends or friends-of-friends. People *believed* in soulmates, and they wanted to help them find each other because it was supposed to make people happy. Connor could understand that. It didn't change the fact he'd prefer people to just not *know*.

Blake sat heavily down on the bench in front of Connor, looking up but fixing his gaze somewhere in the vicinity of Connor's shoulder. He spoke, but Connor couldn't hear him over the voices of the photographers. They were all solemnly promising Hayden that of course, they wouldn't print anything. Several were going through then and there, presumably deleting the images of Connor's soulmark off their cameras.

Sinking into a crouch brought Connor more onto Blake's level. "I'm really sorry," Blake croaked, finally meeting Connor's eyes. "I didn't *mean* to - I was just fooling around, trying to get you back for shoving me."

"Of course you didn't mean it," Connor agreed, though something in his voice sounded almost mechanical. "You couldn't have known I had to go and take the sticker off in the shower." Stupid. It had been *stupid* to forget to replace it. That should have been the first thing Connor had done, he just hadn't thought.

"It'll be alright," Blake promised, and Connor's smile didn't reach his eyes. "No one's going to make a big deal, or be weird." Connor wanted to believe that, he really did, so he nodded.

"Let me drive you home?" Blake offered. "Or buy you a drink. Your choice."

Looking around, Connor could see Hayden ushering the press towards the door. The rest of the Howlers were mostly standing around, finishing getting dressed. There was no chatter, and Connor felt the responsibility for recovery of their good mood settle on *his* shoulders.

"Did we win tonight, or what?" he asked, his voice carrying over the unnatural hush.

"Yeah!" A couple of the guys responded, the others looking startled, but then smiling.

"*Who* won tonight?" Connor asked.

"Howlers!"

"Who'll win the next game?" Connor could feel his body loosening up, lips quirking into a smile.

"Howlers!"

Blake stood up, clapping Connor hard across the shoulders while the rest of the team cheered. They carried on the call and response, voices getting louder and louder. Once again, it was Nilssy's voice that rose above them all.

"Let's get the fuck going, then!"

◆ ◆ ◆

The next morning, staring down at a full-color picture of his soulmark splashed across the front of the sports section, the mood was a lot harder to turn around. Connor's stomach clenched with the certainty that once the name of his soulmate was out in the world, there was no way to call it back.

"I'm sorry, Connor," Coach offered. "I don't know what to tell you. We vetted every man or woman we gave those press credentials to, but I guess the temptation was just too much. We don't even know who leaked it, but we *will* find out. I'm putting a media ban in place, but obviously, that doesn't change the facts. The photo is already all over the internet. Scott's been fielding calls since first thing this morning."

All Connor could do was nod. He'd had to turn his phone off, the notifications from twitter only getting more and more frequent as people woke up to the news. He'd had easily fifty pictures of Ashleys, male and female, sent his way. *Some* had even had legitimate-looking soulmarks of *his* name, though apparently, that wasn't a requirement.

11

"What happens next?" Connor asked, and Coach sighed. It was *uncomfortable* seeing him so serious. He usually joked around as much as any Howler, giving them all shit for not working hard enough. This was different. It made Connor feel almost like a little kid again, watching the adults who were *supposed* to hold his world up falling apart themselves.

"Are you seeing anyone?" Coach asked. "If you are, I suggest giving them a call, -" He didn't need to finish, Connor had already shaken his head. There was one small mercy, at least. He couldn't imagine trying to hold together a relationship while all of Madison was hunting for his soulmate.

"Then other than that, you just wait," Coach carried on. *Waiting* wasn't exactly Connor's strong point. He wanted to *do* something, drive around every store in the city and buy up all the papers, or find a tattoo artist who'd be willing to say it wasn't a *real* soulmark. None of them were *good* plans. If Connor had been able to come up with anything practical, he'd be out doing it, not here listening to Coach tell him to be patient.

"It'll die down," Coach promised, and looked frankly relieved when Connor didn't ask *when*. "I'll tell Tex to up the security checks, make sure you're not getting hassled on your way in or out." He spread his big hands out, in a gesture to indicate there wasn't really anything else that he could do.

Before he left, Connor borrowed the office phone to put through a call to his mom.

"I'm sorry, sweetie," she cooed, "but you never know. Maybe she really will turn up! You'd like to find a girl who was into hockey, wouldn't you?" Connor groaned, not even having the patience left to pretend it wasn't an idiotic thing to say.

"Come on, mom. Would *you* have wanted to be approached by *every* Alex who had even one friend or colleague who was into monster trucks?" he asked. Privately, Connor wondered whether that might have worked out better for his mom than marrying the Alex that she had. He had long ago decided that their divorce - and their relationship post-divorce - was no business of his.

"Well," his mom said, sounding uncertain. "I'm sure it will blow over..." There was a pause, while Connor tried to find something positive to say, before his mom asked, "Do you want me to tell your dad?"

It hurt, more than Connor would have expected it to. It was a reminder that his dad didn't seem to follow *any* of the news stories about what Connor was up to.

"Don't bother," Connor answered. "What's he going to do, anyway?" His mom didn't have an answer for that.

"I wish I were there, sweetie. I'd take you out for pie and ice cream, like when you were little." The memory made Connor smile.

Standing outside the rink, not sure what to do with himself, Connor ended up in his car. He drove through the city until he spotted the kind of little run-down diner he and his mom would've gone to.

He was lucky it was nearly empty. The rink's corner of Madison didn't get a lot of traffic during the day. Anyone who might've recognized him at least had the good sense to leave him alone.

Taking a seat at the bar, Connor looked over the menu while he waited for a waitress to come out of the kitchen. It wasn't a very long wait. A tall brunette, maybe a bit younger than Connor but not by much, came through to give him a smile he only ever saw on waitresses' faces. She looked a great deal more chipper than Connor felt.

She was taller than average, but Connor could easily tell that she was still shorter than him. Most women were. Her brown hair was tied up in a ponytail with some sort of a ribbon, but strands of it still fell loosely, almost as if she couldn't be bothered to properly tie it up. The uniform she was wearing didn't do justice to the curves Connor could tell she had. Still, she looked very attractive, and briefly he was distracted thinking about what she might look like wearing something designed to make her look stunning.

"I recommend the blueberry pancakes," the waitress advised, reaching over the top of Connor's menu to tap her finger against the food in question. Her brown hair fell forward slightly and as Connor's eyes traveled up he had to almost laugh. In some ridiculous cosmic joke scenario, the name tag pinned neatly against her dress read 'Ashley'.

"Yeah?" Connor asked, glancing at the description offered of the pancakes. "I was going to go for cherry pie and chocolate ice cream, but maybe it is a bit early." That had always been his order as a kid, but his nutritionist would definitely advise Connor to skip the heavy pastry, and the cream.

Undecided, Connor looked back up at Ashley. On any normal day, he'd barely even notice that she had the same name as his soulmate. It happened so often, there was no point getting excited about it every single time. Today, Connor wasn't quite sure whether to believe the coincidence was funny or tragic.

"What would you recommend to turn around a really shitty morning?" he asked. "Blueberry pancakes with extra blueberries?"

Ashley, to give her credit, seemed to pause and look at Connor very thoughtfully, as if just staring at him would allow her to bore into his head. Then, after a moment's pause, she gave a nod as if to confirm whatever he'd asked when Connor hadn't asked anything at all.

"Wait here," she told him before disappearing into the kitchen. He didn't have much time to wonder why before she was back, a plate in her hand. Putting it down in front of Connor, Ashley grinned. "Why not both?" She said, pancakes covered in blueberries sitting next to a slice of cherry pie.

Handing Connor some cutlery, Ashley then went to make him a chocolate milkshake. "My duties as a waitress do include asking you if you'd like to talk about why it's been a shitty morning," she advised.

Connor laughed. He immediately tucked into the blueberry pancakes as if he was afraid someone from the team were going to appear at his elbow and take the indulgent feast away from him.

"Do you *like* asking people why they've had shitty mornings?" Connor asked, instead of answering the implied question. He *didn't* particularly want to talk about it. Instead, he was genuinely curious whether Ashley *wanted* to ask, or only felt that she had to. Connor's sister Maisy had worked at a pizza place one summer. As far as Connor had been able to tell, she'd mostly wanted to get customers in and out as quickly as possible so that she could go back to goofing off.

Ashley gave a small shrug at Connor's question. "It's a conversation starter," she said a little teasingly. "And I find that people often love talking about themselves, so asking about their problems makes it seem like good customer service." It kind of made sense, though it did sound a touch disingenuous. As if sensing that thought, Ashley shrugged. "I like hearing about people," she promised.

The way she said it, she made it sound true. It made Connor wonder what other bad days Ashley might've heard about. "I don't know if I'm ready to talk about it," Connor admitted, "but maybe that's all the more reason to practice." Media ban or not, *someone* was going to ask Connor how he felt about the whole mess. He might as well get the awkward stage of not being able to find the right words over with sooner, rather than later.

"The papers printed a picture of my soulmark," he explained. "Literally happened first thing this morning, so it's still kind of overwhelming."

Ashley's eyes widened at the information. It was pretty *significant*. Soulmarks definitely were considered private, but there were plenty of people who wanted to find out what other people's soulmarks were. A perverse sort of pleasure, one that anyone with any sort of celebrity suffered.

"Shit, that sucks," Ashley announced finally. "I'm guessing you're famous then?" She asked before offering Connor somewhat of an apologetic shrug. "I don't recognize you." Which mostly probably just meant that Ashley didn't watch hockey.

"I figured," Connor admitted, with a shrug. "Or at least, I

figured you hadn't seen the picture." He bit down on his lower lip, letting the brief flash of pain distract him from the uncomfortable feeling in his stomach. "You'd probably have said something, seeing as my soulmate's name is Ashley." It didn't feel *good* to tell someone, but it did give Connor at least a small sense of control. He had chosen to tell Ashley, and while he wouldn't have done so under any other circumstances, at least it hadn't been *forced* on him.

Ashley gave a small 'ah', clicking her tongue at the revelation. She didn't actually seem that phased. If she hadn't just told Connor she didn't recognize him, he might've almost thought she had read the papers. Bringing her hand up, Ashley tapped a finger against her name tag. "I get a lot of people telling me they've got my name on them," she commented.

It made Connor frown because even when he had met women called Ashley before, it had never occurred to him to tell them they might be his soulmate. "I understand why it happens," Connor said, perhaps more to himself than to Ashley. "You're pretty, and of course most people want to find their soulmate someday, but it seems really weird to me to make a big deal out of it when they can't even know you."

Taking a bite of the cherry pie, which was delicious, Connor looked back to Ashley. "Do you hate it?" he asked, genuinely curious. Maybe he just didn't like people enough, and that was why it had always bothered him when people wanted to show him his name on them.

"No," Ashley shook her head. "I don't really care. I think it's just an attempt to get me into bed." As Connor had already pointed out, Ashley *was* pretty, so it wasn't very surprising that people would want to. It was a little more surprising that they tried to use *that* as a chat-up line, but then Connor had also been at the receiving end of it.

"Besides," Ashley said drawing his attention back to her. "I'm not a big believer in soulmarks. My parents gave me a common name for a reason." Then, as if it was nothing, Ashley raised her arm and there it was, bare in a way that Connor very rarely saw - her soulmark.

Running down from her elbow in the direction of her wrist, neatly sat the name 'Connor'.

Connor very nearly choked on his pie and had to pound himself on the chest to keep anything from going down the wrong way. He waved off Ashley's concerned move towards him, his eyes still slightly wide. "Sorry," he offered. He couldn't seem to say anything else, his mind simply refusing to move on from the sight of his own name on Ashley's arm.

What were the chances? Connor had never been very good at math, but he was sure they had to be pretty slim. Granted, neither Connor nor Ashley were *rare* names, not like someone's chances of getting matched with a Braxton or a Perpetua. To meet an Ashley who had his name as her soulmark on the same day his own had been revealed seemed... extraordinary.

"You might not believe this now," Connor said, feeling faintly sheepish he hadn't mentioned it earlier, "but I'm Connor Lewis. I can show you my driver's license and everything."

"Seriously?" Ashley asked, sounding like she *was* suspicious of the convenience of Connor's name being the same as the name on her arm. But she also didn't take him up on his offer to show her his driver's license to prove it. Instead, Ashley shrugged. "It's also a pretty common name," she commented. "Did your parents give you a common name intentionally? Mine did."

The question genuinely made Connor pause before he shook his head. His parents' relationship was another of those things Connor didn't really talk about. In a way, telling Ashley his soulmate's name had already ripped the band-aid off.

"No, it wasn't deliberate," he answered. "My parents thought they were soulmates when I was born, I don't think they'd have wanted to make it hard for me." Certainly, his mom wouldn't have wanted to. Connor was never very sure *what* his dad felt about anything.

"What would your parents have done if your soulmark had ended up reading Hepzibah, or something?" he asked. "Not too many of those around." Unlike Connor, of which there were plenty. Something Connor often told the hockey fans who so badly *wanted* him to be their soulmate.

"I would still wear it openly," Ashley shrugged in response. "It probably would have been rarer to meet someone with that name." The way Ashley said it sounded so... unbothered. Some people didn't care about soulmarks, there were even campaigns and self-help books. Connor had never *met* someone who agreed with them.

Leaning against the counter, Ashley glanced down at her soulmark, now partially hidden by the sleeve of her dress. "People put too much worth on the soulmarks. Relationships should be about getting on, about working together not about just having someone's name on you."

"Absolutely," Connor agreed, his own gaze also drawn to the 'NNOR' he could still see on Ashley's arm. It *didn't* make him think that Ashley ought to be his soulmate. He didn't want to get her number 'just in case', date her just because their names were right.

It *did* make Connor think about how convenient it would be if he could've pointed the press at someone like Ashley. He could tell them that he'd already found the person of his dreams and didn't need any help looking for her.

Thoughtfully, Connor chewed through another bite of pancake, before waving the fork in Ashley's direction. "I promise, this is not about me hitting on you," he prefaced, "but are you seeing anyone at the moment?"

Ashley raised an eyebrow at him, and Connor couldn't blame her. It *did* sound like he was hitting on her. "I feel that my answer should depend on whatever the next question you're planning to ask is," she said a little teasingly but did also shake her head. "I'm single."

It seemed like too good an opportunity to pass up. Here was an Ashley, whose soulmate was a Connor, and who also wasn't particularly caught up in the idea of soulmates and coincidences. Connor could hardly imagine a *more* perfect person to keep the press off his back, at least until the uproar died down.

If Ashley had been dying to meet The One, Connor wouldn't have asked her, but she *wasn't*. Still, he hesitated. Throwing someone else to the press, even in a limited way, was a lot to ask. "I play for the Howlers," Connor explained, "and the papers getting hold of my soulmark means our PR team is being bombarded with Ashleys all over Wisconsin who want to meet me. We can't reply to all of them, and if I ignore them, they'll just keep emailing, or they'll start turning up at games, and that's even more of a security risk."

He paused, to see if Ashley was following, and she gave him a small wave, encouraging him to keep going. "If I could put out one press release, saying I've already found my Ashley, and no others need to apply... I think people would respect that." Ashley must *know* that her views about soulmarks not mattering were rare. As much as Connor would've liked to just tell people he wasn't looking to date right now, he didn't trust it would work.

He shot Ashey a cheeky grin, as he came to the crux of his question. "So, Ashley, I guess I'm asking if you want to be my girlfriend. For a little while, just until the fuss dies down."

CHAPTER TWO

Ashley

Growing up, Ashley Walton's parents had always been very insistent about telling her how soulmarks did not *decide* what her life should be like. Their own didn't match and it wasn't until Ashley had started secondary school that she truly understood how *different* that was from a lot of other people. For a while, Ashley had worried that her parents weren't *really* happy, but it was a worry that she'd quickly got over.

Levi and Holly Walton were the happiest couple Ashley had ever met. Her parents were the proof - at least to Ashley - that soulmarks didn't *matter*. Her mom had never tried to *hide* her soulmark, the name 'Ansel' sitting against her hip, but it had also always been easy to cover it with clothes. Levi had chosen to wear a sticker over 'Gertrude' but only because it made others uncomfortable, those who knew his wife was called Holly.

Ashley's upbringing, even if some would describe it as odd, had given her a lot of confidence in herself. She had never been in a position where she felt like she *had to* find a soulmate. Doing things that made her happy, *that* was what her parents raised her to believe was important. Thus, when Ashley's soul-mark came through aged eight - unusually young - she didn't *want* to hide it.

'Connor' had always sat snugly against Ashley's arm and yes, every so often she'd meet someone who'd say 'hey that's my name'. On a few occasions, it had even been someone who carried Ashley's name, too. They all seemed equally puzzled when Ashley said she didn't want to date them just because they could be soulmates. It was less common nowadays that people dated just because the other person carried their name, but it was certainly still prevalent enough.

It wasn't something Ashley felt she was missing out on. She *liked* that she could date whoever. She especially liked that the guys who wanted to date her equally didn't tend to care about soulmarks because Ashley's was so exposed it was hard to not know what it said.

Working as a waitress came with a lot of people telling Ashley they had her name on them. It also came with an equal number of people asking her out - some of whom carried her name and some of whom didn't. Ashley was used to turning such offers down quickly and easily, but she had to admit that being asked to be someone's fake girlfriend was... new.

At least the guy was attractive. Even with him seated, Ashley could tell that Connor was well built. His shoulders were wide, with arms to match. Ashley didn't get to see a lot of guys at the diner who looked like they regularly worked out, so this one stood out even more so.

His face was attractive, too. A jawline that looked as if it had been shaped specifically to be attractive. The blue of his eyes stood out somehow even more against the tanned skin. His hair was probably the one thing Ashley felt might use some fixing, a shaggy mess of light brown sticking out in every direction.

"You want me to be your PR girlfriend?" Ashley asked frowning at Connor. "That is your top plan? Meet a waitress at a diner, ask her to be your pretend girlfriend? What if I went to the papers with *that*?" She wasn't going to but Jesus, really?

Shaking her head, Ashley gave Connor another, rather serious look. "It certainly seems like you need help," she didn't add 'because you're an idiot', but Ashley felt it was definitely implied. "How would this even work? It seems a bit... weird."

"Okay," Connor agreed, looking sheepish, "it's possible that 'plan' is too generous a description. It was more... an idea. I haven't really thought it through." That much, Ashley felt, was rather obvious, but she didn't say so, instead giving Connor time *to* think it through. She was not going to agree until he'd actually explained what he wanted.

"Like I said, a press release, and we could go on a few dates, get our pictures taken together. You'd definitely get some attention from the press, so I'll get it if you don't want to do this." He shrugged. "I'm sure we can think of something you can get out of it. I'm not asking you to do it just because it'd be convenient for me."

Ashley *assumed* that what Connor was implying was a financial something that she would be getting out of it. Frankly, Ashley supposed she could use the money. He wouldn't be wrong in presuming that she'd need it working mid-morning shifts at a diner. What Ashley was actually more interested in was all this PR talk.

Working in a diner was not Ashley's dream job, hardly. In fact, it wasn't really much else than a pocket money job while she studied at college. It was her last year, doing a Master's in Public Relations, so yeah, the PR stuff? Ashley was quite interested in that.

"If I was to do this - and I'm not saying that I will," Ashley started, making very sure Connor knew she wasn't agreeing *yet*. "Could I do your PR for this?" It was definitely a weird request and Ashley rushed in to add, "That's what I'm studying. I'm a few months away from finishing my Master's in Public Relations and this, well, this would make for a pretty great final thesis."

Well, it really *would*. And Connor was hardly unattractive, Ashley could do worse for a college project and a fake boyfriend.

Connor didn't answer at once. Ashley had to give him credit that at least he didn't seem desperate, willing to promise her anything just to get her to agree. "We'd have to talk to the team about that," he finally said. "I can't really give away bits of Scott's job without at least asking him first. *I've* got no objections, though." He gave Ashley a smile, like he trusted her already, which was flattering, if not very wise.

"I can step out and give them a call now?" Connor suggested, and then glanced down at his half-eaten pile of blueberry pancakes. "Well, in a few minutes," he amended. "If Scott says you can do the PR, what else do we need to talk about before you make a decision?"

Ashley let Connor eat as she thought about his question. If she *was* actually going to do this - and that was still a big *if* - there'd definitely need to be some set... rules, she supposed. "We'd need to figure out some sort of relationship history," she commented. "How long have we dated? How did we meet?" That one was pretty obvious actually. "Here, we would've met here. Keep things as close to the truth as possible."

"It'd have to be longer than... a few weeks, otherwise none of the Ashleys currently trying to get in touch will believe you haven't just chosen *badly*." Which obviously Connor had done, but Ashley felt they could very easily work around that. "How often would we need to see each other? Would I be required to attend your games? I should. What about public engagements, do you even have those?" Ashley really wasn't sure *how* that side of hockey worked (or frankly, any side). "I'm going to have to learn the rules of hockey."

There were a lot of other questions Ashley had, but she did pause to let Connor get a word in edgewise.

"You don't even know the rules?" Connor asked, eyebrows shooting up into his hairline. "It's not complicated. I can explain it over lunch or something before you come to a game."

He paused, tongue darting out over his lip to collect a crumb of pastry. "You answered most of your own questions," he teased, "but yeah, we have some public events. There's a fan tour," Connor he listed, "but you wouldn't have to come to that. People don't usually bring their girlfriends, because it's just not much fun for them. Lots of signing autographs and answering questions, giving out free t-shirts..." He shrugged, and his smile didn't quite reach his eyes. It made Ashley wonder whether *he* found it fun.

"Next month we've got a big fund-raising gala type thing," he went on to explain. "It's a different charity every year. We get dressed up, eat fancy food, talk hockey with a bunch of people who are likely to donate to whatever the cause is. There's some dancing." He looked at Ashley, narrowing his blue eyes slightly. "Can you dance?"

"Yeah, I can dance," Ashley nodded. She couldn't say she'd been to a *gala* before but she had taken formal dancing as a kid, so she could hold her own.

The question was, was she really going to do *this*? Some random guy comes into the diner she works in and asks her to be his pretend girlfriend? More than that, his pretend *soulmate*. "Who would know? Like that this isn't *real*?" Ashley asked, the thought really only now occurring her.

"My mom," Connor answered, without even pausing for breath. "And my sister. Scott, he's the Howler's PR." He paused, swirling his straw slowly in his milkshake while he considered. "Probably the Howler's coach. He's pretty concerned about the whole situation, I think he'd feel better knowing I wasn't outing a real relationship that I'd been trying to keep private."

It surprised Ashley that none of the people Connor listed were his team, but who was she to question it? Except, Ashley supposed, she *was* his fake girlfriend. It did make her think, dates or not, they'd have to at least appear like they knew each other well.

"Why not your team?" She asked because Ashley *wanted* to know. And yeah, maybe it was also a bit of a test to see how honest Connor was with his answer. They didn't know each other and Ashley felt that if they were going to lie to people together, they should be honest with each other.

Connor didn't reply immediately, though he opened his mouth once or twice, as if he was about to say something. Finally, he sighed. "Seriously, I just don't want to put up with the *shit* they'll give me," he admitted. "I love them, and they'd *get* it, but they'd still tease me endlessly." He shrugged.

"On top of that, it just seems like the fewer people know, the smaller the chance it'll get out. No one on the team will feel betrayed if they find out I was lying. Mom would, so I have to tell her the truth."

That *was* a good answer, in Ashley's opinion anyway. It certainly didn't imply that she should say no to this ridiculous idea straight out. There was also something just *nice* in having Connor say he couldn't and wouldn't lie to his mom. Ashley had always been close to her parents, so she liked that. Given, if they would go ahead with this, Ashley had no intention of telling *her* parents the truth. It'd be easier to just say she wasn't sure if Connor was her true soulmate. Her parents certainly would be fine with it.

"So what is it that you actually would want me to do? I don't have to move in with you or something, do I?" Because that'd definitely be a no-no, Ashley's cat wouldn't like that.

Connor's eyes widened as he shook his head. "Fuck no, I'm not ready for a girlfriend I *live with*. Even a pretend one." He finished his pie, pushing the plate back towards Ashley with a smile. "We don't have to say we've been dating *that* long. It can be a few months. Long enough that it's not brand new, not so long we're looking at apartments together."

That didn't really answer Ashley's question of what she *would* have to do, but Connor carried on. "I guess... come to games, be seen around with me. Holding hands, that kind of thing. We don't have to make out for the cameras. Some of the guys do, but just as many don't."

"Okay," Ashley said before she could think better of it. There weren't any glaring reasons to say *no*. Apart from how this was definitely one of the strangest things to happen to her. Still, it would make *such* a good research project and if Ashley spun this the right way? She could probably make it look pretty good on her CV. Working PR for an NHL team would get her far.

Taking the now empty plate, Ashley took it through to the back, giving herself a small moment to think all of this through. Frankly, she figured, even if this did come out for what it truly was, Ashley couldn't see how *she* would lose out. Not that there was really any way it would. They could just say that it turned out they *weren't* soulmates. It happened plenty, especially for people with names as common as theirs.

When she returned, Ashley gave Connor a look. "Alright, so what next?"

It seemed to take Connor a moment to realize she was *agreeing*. When he did, Connor gave her a brilliant smile, making him look almost a different person than he had when he'd come in. "I guess now I ask Scott whether he's willing to let you handle the PR on this. Maybe the team can treat it like an internship, make it seem a bit more respectable?" The uncertain tone made Ashley realize that Connor knew as much about PR as she did about hockey. Well, they were probably both going to learn something, if nothing else.

"Who would you want to know the truth?" he asked. "That seems like the first thing Scott's going to ask me." He paused, clearly suppressing a chuckle. "Or second, after how I know you're not a lunatic fan."

"No one," Ashley shook her head. "No one I know is going to think it weird that I have a new boyfriend, even if our soulmarks match." It was true, really. Ashley's parents probably wouldn't even find out since they didn't follow sports or gossip therein, and her friends would just... not mind. It seemed a lot easier than explaining that she'd agreed to fake date a complete stranger.

Connor looked briefly surprised, but after a moment he nodded. "Alright, that's fair. Are there any events you want *me* to come to, or will it be less weird if we keep out of your life as much as we can?" He frowned slightly, and Ashley wondered if the weirdness of the suggestion was just hitting him *now*.

If so, he didn't back down, instead pulling his phone from his jacket pocket, unlocking it and offering it to Ashley. "You'd better give me your number," he said, lightly. "Otherwise I won't be able to call you for dates."

Taking the phone, Ashley shook her head. "You're welcome to come to whatever stuff with me, but honestly, I don't get up to much. Mostly studying and working, an occasional party here or there." Truthfully, Ashley couldn't even think of anything that she had planned, which probably made her sound pretty lame. Studying did keep her busy and that was hardly *embarrassing*.

"I can come to a party," Connor agreed, with a grin. "I'm not much help at studying, and I guess your boss would prefer I didn't hang around here all the time. Not to mention, that's probably *weird*."

It would be weird, but Ashley was pretty sure her boss would love having one of Madison Howlers hang out at the diner. Not that Ashley planned to tell either Connor *or* Warren that was an option.

Once she'd saved her number in Connor's phone, Ashley turned the camera on before taking a selfie of herself smiling widely. "Best make that your lock screen image," she advised. "We're probably going to need more. Have you got an Instagram?"

Taking his phone back, and ignoring the many notification alerts, Connor swiped through to set a new lock screen, then to his Instagram. "It's mostly pictures of the Howlers," he said, unapologetically, "and whatever Scott schedules for me to post. Is this the kind of thing you study, then? How to get followers and do all the hashtags properly?"

"Not exactly, but yeah we did have a class on that." There were a lot more things, but Ashley couldn't deny that figuring out how social media could be utilized was a pretty significant part of a PR job.

It seemed pretty obvious to Ashley that if they were going to do this - and apparently they were - she was going to have to be the one who made sure they did this right. That, to be fair, suited her well. Ashley *enjoyed* taking the lead on things, though she did recognize that you couldn't just lead a relationship, even a fake one.

"Have whoever does your PR - Scott? - put out a press release that you have found your soulmate. It's nice and flattering to have so many people step forward but none of them are *the* Ashley," she listed, before fetching a piece of paper to write it all out as bullet points. Maybe she could include this in her essay, too.

Handing the list of immediate actions to Connor, Ashley gave him a wide smile. "Pick me up at six? My address is on the paper."

Glancing down, Connor read over what Ashley had written, tapping a finger idly against her address. When he looked up, he raised an eyebrow at her. "Is our date going to be this efficient?"

The frown on Ashley's face clearly rushed Connor to add that he didn't mind. Being efficient was just the way Ashley *was*. She liked planning things, having plans and a clear idea of things. It was on the tip of her tongue to say that if Connor wasn't okay with that, this wouldn't work out. Except he didn't say that.

"I usually have to do all the work on dates, deciding where to go, and where there won't be too many journalists." He smiled like a thought was just occurring to him. "We can go somewhere that's actually *cool*!"

The ease with which Connor said it'd be nice for someone else to decide was... surprising. Ashley was so used to guys telling her she was *too bossy* or *too organized* that it genuinely was novel to find someone who didn't straight away tell her that. It felt... kind of nice, really.

"What's cool?" She asked suspiciously. Maybe Ashley should've asked about Connor's date ideas first.

"There's supposedly a bar that's got ping pong tables," Connor answered, "and they make a Bloody Mary using their own brand of hot sauce. All the reviews say it's incredible. The team keep saying we'll all go down there one night, but it hasn't happened yet."

As if he felt he had to justify that, Connor added. "We usually only all go out together after games, and then we've got our traditions. We can't just mix it up and go somewhere new - we might ruin the luck!"

Ashley took a moment before she responded to that, mostly because... if she had had to write a response she imagined a professional athlete to give to 'what is cool to you', it'd be that. Drinking spicy drinks that he normally didn't get to. Not that Ashley had expected the answer to be a *museum* or anything, but still. A bar wasn't what she had been aiming for but it'd serve its purpose.

"Alright, I guess we'll go drink spicy Bloody Maries." There was no reason for them *not to* and Ashley kind of caught herself thinking that she wanted to see Connor do something he liked. It was boding well for the fake-dating (which she probably needed to start thinking of as actual dating in her head).

"Great!" Connor said, grinning like he was genuinely excited about the prospect. Once he'd paid for his meal, he did sober a little. "Thank you, for agreeing to do this," he said. "I know you'll be getting something out of it, too, but it's still a lot of hassle to go through for a stranger. I don't want you to think I don't appreciate it."

Ashley was a little surprised by how *honest* Connor sounded, but then, she also hadn't really looked up just how much damage the revelation of his soulmark had done on the internet. Not that having a name as generic as 'Ashley' should really matter (but perhaps it made it worse because it invited *everyone* called Ashley to throw themselves at him).

"Make a list," Ashley told Connor before he could leave. "Make a list of things you'd expect to know about a girlfriend after three months of dating and I'll just... tell you. If we're going to make this seem plausible, we're going to have to get to know each other."

It was going to be *interesting* and honestly, right now Ashley didn't have a lot of interesting things going on, so *why not?*

She did somewhat suspect that that was also what a lot of terrible things started with - the sort of confidently asked 'why not?'.

CHAPTER THREE

Connor

S cott had been surprisingly willing to take Ashley on as a sort of unofficial intern. It suggested, at least to Connor, that his idea of a fake girlfriend must've been a good one. His mom had been excited, too, especially since Ashley's soulmark matched his name. Maisy had been less certain, but she *had* approved of Ashley's suggestion that Connor made a list of things he thought he'd know about a girlfriend after three months.

Connor had started with basic things - favorite food, favorite movie - before realizing it was unlikely a reporter would ever think to ask him about those. He tried to remember what he'd known about girlfriends he'd actually been with for three months. It wasn't something that had happened recently. Connor liked dates, what he didn't like were all the *complications*. Most girlfriends tended to get complicated before three months, at least in Connor's experience.

This would be different. Connor had spent half the afternoon swiping through notifications on twitter, changing his settings so that people couldn't contact him unless he actually knew them. He'd become more and more convinced that telling people he already *had* a girlfriend was the best way to go. It would get the pressure off him, and off Scott, without making thousands of fans feel like he'd jilted them. Besides, Ashley seemed cool, and she was walking into this with her eyes open. Connor felt a lot better about that than he would about dating someone who thought he genuinely wanted her to be his soulmate.

He had to admit, walking into the bar with Ashley on his arm had felt pretty fucking good. She looked *gorgeous* out of her waitress uniform, with her hair falling loose to her shoulders. People definitely stopped and noticed them when they walked in. Connor had booked them a table near the bar. They'd covered a lot of the basics over their first glasses of Bloody Mary - names and ages of siblings, where they'd both grown up.

As their second drinks arrived, Connor asked, "How do you like to celebrate birthdays?" It was something that had definitely tripped him up with women before. "As in," he clarified, "what do you *actually* want, not just what do you tell people you want. It's no good you telling me you don't want a big fuss if you actually do."

"Why would I tell people something different from how I actually want to celebrate my birthday?" Ashley asked with a frown. "Anyway, I actually do like my birthdays and I like a fuss," she answered not giving Connor an opportunity to answer her question first. Ashley reached to take another sip of her Bloody Mary and scrunched her nose up the same way she had done every single time before. Yet, she had also ordered it *again*, so Connor didn't think she *hated* it.

His eyes followed her fingers as they tugged a strand of stray hair behind her ear. "Last year my friends organized a Murder Mystery for my birthday, that was pretty fun until it turned out that I was the victim."

"So, what, you just had to lie there pretending to be dead, while they did all the solving?" Connor asked, frowning so hard he could feel his brow wrinkling. "That sounds *shit*." Connor wasn't really sure how a for-fun Murder Mystery worked, but he wouldn't have thought you even needed a real person to play the body. "Did you get up and haunt them, and give them terrible clues about what had actually happened? That's what I would've done."

"I was allowed to walk around and give bad clues," Ashley nodded. "But I think I still would've preferred to be *alive* for my own birthday party." That seemed like a fair enough wish and not *quite* what Connor had thought of when he'd said 'fuss'.

A Murder Mystery was very *different* from what most of Connor's previous girlfriends had apparently wanted. Their versions of 'enough fuss' tended to involve exclusive restaurants and nice presents. "Haven't you ever been with someone who said they didn't want you to bother, then got annoyed when you just did something low-key?" Connor asked. He felt sure it wasn't an experience only he had ever had.

"No, not really," Ashley shrugged in response. "Maybe it's more of a thing if you date girls? I haven't ever dated girls." She didn't seem very *bothered* by not having had the experience of either dating girls or dating someone who was confused about what they wanted.

Setting her glass down again, Ashley gave Connor a look that almost seemed like she was planning to read how truthful his answer to her next question was, "What about you, then? Do you like to be fussed over?"

"Of course," Connor answered. "It's not that I don't understand why people *want* a fuss. It just makes my head ache that they won't *say* so." Maybe it was a girl thing, though Maisy would definitely punch Connor if she ever heard him suggest that. Luckily, she didn't punch very hard. "I like breakfast in bed if I don't have training, and I'll usually book a VIP section in a club for me and the team."

He paused, taking a sip of his drink and enjoying the level of spice as it burned along his nerve-endings. "You should probably know that the team *are* my friends, pretty much. We spend so much time together, it's hard for them not to be. Even most of the friends I had in high school played hockey, so they've moved to where ever they got job offers." Not *all* of Connor's friends had been good enough to play pro - but the ones that hadn't were the ones Connor didn't see much these days. "Some people find it weird, but it's just the way hockey *is*."

If Ashley *did* find it weird, she didn't say as much or look like she did. Instead, she just shrugged and reached for her drink. "So how are you going to explain to them that you've dated someone for three months and haven't told them?" She asked.

It was a good question, and Connor found it quite *sweet* how Ashley seemed to be concerned about his relationship with the team. It was also an easy question to answer. "I'll just tell them that you could be my soulmate, and I wanted to see how it went before I shared it with the world." Connor had never dated an Ashley, and he'd certainly never looked for one. If, by chance, he met one that he liked, he *did* think the added pressure would make him more hesitant than he might be with just any other girl.

Thinking about it, Connor wondered what he was going to tell his team when he and Ashley 'broke up'. That was not today's problem. "Are you still friends with your exes?" Connor asked since that was another question on his list. "I'm not, but I won't be weird about it if you are."

Connor's promise made Ashley laugh and she shook her head. "I'm friendly with some of them, I've never had an *awful* break-up," Ashley explained. That seemed like a pretty good thing so Connor nodded.

"Alright, so should we discuss just how we're doing this?" Ashley asked. They'd gone over the lists (because she'd made one, too) and were now caught up on stuff like how long they had dated (three months), where they met (the diner) and whether they wanted a fuss on their birthdays (yes). "It would be good for me to come to your next game, I've given a quick read to the Wiki page on ice hockey. You might still want to run over the rules with me and maybe show me a YouTube video or something."

Ashley's organization and planning were really quite impressive. "Oh, and do you have a jersey with your name I can have? What good girlfriend wouldn't wear one of those, right?"

"Right," Connor agreed and had to take a sip of his drink to distract himself from the sudden mental image of Ashley in his Howlers' jersey and *nothing else.* It didn't really work, probably because alcohol only made him feel more relaxed about such thoughts. With an effort, Connor managed to focus on the conversation at hand.

Showing Ashley some ice hockey highlights was definitely something Connor felt equipped to do, and he nodded. "You can come back to mine after this?" he suggested. "It's going to look a bit weird if I drop you back off at your place. I assume after three months, you'd be spending some nights."

Ashley raised her eyebrow at Connor at the suggestion that she come back to his. Something about his explanation must've sounded reasonable enough, though, because she didn't challenge it. She just took another sip of her drink, her nose scrunching up just as Connor had come to expect it to. It was a weird, yet oddly endearing, reaction to spice.

"Alright, but to learn about hockey, not anything else," she specified.

It made Connor raise an eyebrow back at her before he laughed. "Of course," he assured. "I promise, this is not an exceptionally weird and long-winded way to get you into bed." How would that even work? Connor had heard of guys going to exceptional lengths, but anything that relied on finding someone with a specific soulmark just seemed unrealistically complicated.

"You don't have to stay the whole night," he added because he had actually thought about this. "If you come in, stay for a while to watch some videos, then you can get an Uber home." Reporters were not going to camp outside Connor's apartment to make sure his girlfriend wasn't secretly leaving in the middle of the night. He wasn't *that* famous. Besides, why would anybody think she *would* be?

Thinking of hockey, Connor was reminded that Ashley

had been in Madison for nearly three years, and had somehow never seen a hockey game. "Have you been deliberately avoiding hockey?" he asked.

"No, of course not," Ashley said shaking her head. "I just..." The sentence sort of trailed off and Ashley shrugged. "I didn't grow up with hockey. I used to play soccer in school. My dad always liked football, hockey just wasn't something I was raised with so I haven't had any real interest in watching it." It all sounded very reasonable, even if Connor felt that never having seen a hockey game was a sad state of affairs.

Hockey had *very much* been something that Connor was raised with, to the extent that it was genuinely difficult for him to imagine the world any other way. "It's quite aggressive," he warned, though Wikipedia would likely have already given Ashley an idea of that. "So I guess you probably need to know how you'd feel about watching a boyfriend get slammed into the side of the rink."

From what he knew of her, Connor didn't think Ashley was going to be one of those girls who found it all very upsetting, which was good. There was just no way Connor could've worked out with someone who spent every match worrying he was going to get hurt.

"Well, it doesn't sound *ideal* but it's your job," Ashley commented. "Besides, it's *sports*, I might not know hockey but I get that sports can be pretty brutal." She really didn't seem that bothered and it was kind of nice that despite not knowing hockey, Ashley was still willing to learn. Obviously, Connor would want to have a girlfriend who was interested in learning the rules of hockey for him. Having a fake girlfriend who did seemed... somehow even more special, in a strange sort of way.

"When is your next game?" Ashley asked. "It can be our first outing. Or whatever. Do I just watch the game and go home? I assume you go out after the game to celebrate or something?" The implication that the Howlers would win was also one that Connor appreciated.

Despite having had girlfriends who lived in the city, it

had been a while since anyone had come to see Connor play. He didn't attempt to hide his enjoyment of the thought. "It's next week," he answered, eagerly. "Will it be weird if I share my calendar with you? It seems… easier." It also seemed kind of intimate, in a way Connor was usually hesitant to be with girlfriends.

"You can come along to the celebrations," he offered. "It will be rowdy, but you don't seem like a delicate flower who can't handle it." There were definitely girls who were. Connor was always slightly surprised that his teammates wanted to date them, but of course, it was none of his business.

Ashley gave a startled laugh at that and whilst Connor didn't know why it was funny, he grinned back anyway. "Sure, share your calendar with me and I'll come to your after game party or whatever." The easiness with which Ashley just *agreed* was really nice and her smile was definitely infectious, making Connor grin back.

"Alright. One more Bloody Mary each and then you can take me home and show me some hockey highlights," Ashley announced, smacking her now-empty glass down on the table with gusto.

After the press release, things hadn't died down quite as much as Connor had expected. There'd been fewer DMs with photos of people's soulmarks, but *so many* people congratulating him on finally meeting *the one*, and still more who sent him lists of why they would be the *better* Ashley. Scott had seemed as surprised as Connor, but Ashley had just shrugged and said they needed to go somewhere public on a date.

Connor could hardly object to that, especially not when Ashley suggested an amusement park. Connor loved roller coasters, but he didn't often get to go, and driving Ashley out on sunny Saturday had been exciting, and companionable. Once they'd arrived, she'd taken Connor's hand, leaning in so he could

Camellia Tate

snap a selfie of them both for his Instagram. If anything, Ashley looked even more beautiful than she had on their first date. Connor couldn't help noticing the warmth of her hand in his, and how good her hair smelled.

As they walked towards the first of the rides, Ashley didn't let go, so Connor gave her hand a squeeze. "Is this good material for your thesis?" he asked. Having never been to college, Connor honestly didn't know much about it

"It kind of is, yes," Ashley nodded, her tone somewhat amused. "This should be a good place for us. There's plenty of exposure, everyone's taking pictures but also somewhere to escape if we need to." At that Ashley nodded her head toward the rides and Connor had to admit, it certainly *seemed* well thought out.

"It's interesting. I do know it's less so for you, but I've never dated someone famous, it's... different." As if on cue someone stepped in their way then to ask Connor for an autograph and a selfie.

Connor smiled, posing for the picture and obligingly scrawling his signature across the front of a notebook. Like always, he wished he knew what to *say*, but at least little kids didn't seem to mind if he was quiet.

"I've never dated someone famous, either," Connor quipped, returning to their conversation once they resumed their walk. "I don't know how I'd feel if it was you getting stopped all the time, rather than me." Maybe that would be easier. "What do you find interesting about it?"

"It's just different, isn't it?" Ashley commented. "The whole soulmate thing is hard for a lot of people anyway, all the pressure to meet 'the One'." She supplied the air quotes with her free hand, waving it in the air. "But being in the public eye? It's that much more difficult. Like with you and everyone knowing your soulmate's name and claiming - or offering - to be it."

The mention of it made Connor glance down to their linked hands. Ashley had worn a dress that had a sleeve finishing just short of her elbow, exposing the name against her arm for everyone to see. It was *rare* to see someone so openly showing it off, even if they did think they'd met their true soulmate.

"People also look up to you, expect your love story to somehow be... more, I guess?" She continued, not noticing Connor's gaze. "All of that's just very interesting. From a sociological point of view."

Connor had never really thought about it that way, but what Ashley said made sense. He was used to being asked questions about how he trained, or how he'd gotten signed to the Howlers. It made sense to him that people who wanted to play pro hockey would ask for *those* tips, even though he didn't have much useful advice. That someone might look up to how he *dated* was definitely a new perspective.

"You make it sound interesting," Connor said, with a smile down at Ashley. "It's never occurred to me to wonder *why* people always want to know what celebrities are up to, but when you explain it, it makes sense." Connor couldn't help respecting Ashley for that. It wasn't everyone who could explain something so well in so few words.

"Is that how you decided to study PR, then?" he asked. "You wanted to do something related to sociology? I kind of assumed most PR assistants just wanted to hang out with famous people. Maybe that wasn't very fair." Ashley was definitely making Connor reconsider.

Ashley laughed, giving his hand a small tug. "Well, I'm obviously only here for your celebrity," she teased, though it was odd to think that she *wasn't*. Or to consider how different this would've been if Connor had asked one of his *fans* to do this for him. Almost as if sensing that perhaps her joke hadn't gone down that well, Ashley tugged on Connor's hand lightly.

"I like PR because it lets me learn how people think. How to present a thing to make it seem a specific way," she explained. "So yeah, I guess it's fair to say that sort of is why I picked it as a subject. If it makes you feel better, I can say I just want to make famous people's lives better?" Ashley offered with a grin.

Appreciating the attempt, Connor smiled back. "You're

definitely making my life better," he agreed, genuinely grateful. Not only had the press release reduced the number of fans desperate to be Connor's one true love, but spending time with Ashley was actually *enjoyable*. Connor hadn't quite expected that when he'd asked her if she'd be his fake girlfriend. "I mean, you brought me to an amusement park," he teased. "Who doesn't love that?"

Though *he* hadn't been to college, Connor knew people who had, and people who'd dropped out. Ashley obviously wasn't one of those. "Is it everything you expected it to be?" he asked. And then, to clarify, added, "The studying, I mean. Did you do a lot of research so you knew what you were getting into?" Connor was starting to understand that Ashley was not a person who did things spontaneously. That kind of made him want to surprise her with something, just to see what she was like *without* a plan.

"I did do a lot of research, yes. I like... planning," there was hesitation in her description and Connor didn't really know *why*. Ashley brushed past it quickly enough. "I've even got a job lined up," she said, making Connor give her a curious look before she continued.

"It's in Dallas, working for a big brand, starting once I graduate in a few months' time." Ashley *sounded* excited, if perhaps a little cautious. Connor was quickly learning that she was just someone who approached things carefully.

Though he smiled, Connor felt a little sad to think Ashley wouldn't be around in Madison for much longer. Of course, he didn't want to carry on a fake relationship for longer than he *had* to. Maybe Connor should've felt relieved there was a hard out. It would save a lot of questions about their 'break-up'.

"That's pretty far away," he observed. "Are you looking forward to it? Whole new place, and all that?" Some people did like moving. For Connor, it had always been more of a necessary evil. Getting picked to play for his home team growing up had been an impossible dream. Connor had lived in Madison long enough now to consider it almost-home.

"I am excited," Ashley smiled. "It's... different, challenging. But mostly, I'm excited not to work in a diner anymore." Her tone was definitely joking, but Connor could also see how that was probably *true*. If she wanted to work in PR, her job in a diner wasn't going to get there.

Another person stopped them to ask Connor for an autograph and Ashley smiled. "Go ahead," she encouraged taking her hand back and Connor felt almost a sudden loss. It made it even harder than usual to concentrate on engaging with the fan.

A picture and an autograph later, Connor turned back to Ashley. "You should win me a bear," she informed him, waving her hand towards one of the amusement park games.

It surprised a laugh out of Connor because it seemed such a high-school-boyfriend thing to do. "I would be delighted," he told Ashley, genuinely meaning it. He *liked* the idea of photographs being taken of Ashley holding an oversized bear that he'd won her. "But don't you know these games are rigged?" he teased, sure that Ashley knew that even better than he did.

Connor wasn't going to let that stop him. Ashley wanted a bear, and he would get her one. He paid for five balls. The object of the game was to knock over all the plastic bottles to win the big prize. "Do you keep sentimental things like this?" he asked, waving a hand at the displayed soft toys, and realizing it was something that he ought to know about his 'girlfriend'. "Or is the poor bear going to end up in a thrift store by this time next week?"

"Not by the end of the *week*," Ashley shook her head. "Maybe end of the month," she added teasingly. The way she teased was nice. Connor was used to hockey chirps, this felt quite different. Yet also a little similar in how it was *friendly*. "I'd keep it if it's small, I'm not keeping one of the huge ones. So, I guess, don't win big?"

Connor rolled his eyes. "You have clearly never dated an athlete," he teased back. "What's the point of competing if you're not trying to win as big as possible? Even if we only need to win by one goal to qualify, we always play to win until the very end. At least, on the Howlers." Some teams played more defensively, but Connor loved being on the attack.

He focused his considerable attention on the pyramid of bottles, hurling the ball straight for the middle. With a crash, the top levels toppled over, but the bottom row barely moved. With his second ball, Connor took out the left-hand side, from bottom to top, but it still wasn't enough to win big.

Finally, narrowing his eyes and adjusting his aim, Connor knocked down the entire pyramid, his eyes lighting up as the stall-worker's voice rose above the crowd. "And we have a winner! Congratulations, sir, and here's your prize for the lovely lady."

Connor couldn't help laughing, seeing Ashley reluctantly wrap her arms around the giant blue teddy bear, hoisting it against her hip. "Smile for the cameras," he teased, draping an arm over her shoulders because people *were* indeed snapping pictures left and right.

Ashley *did* smile for the camera, but she also bumped the head of the bear against Connor. "Thank you, baby, it's all I ever dreamt of," Ashley announced loudly before turning the bear to have it look at her and then back to look at Connor. "I'm going to name him Banshee," she informed Connor. "Because they howl. Get it?" Ashley certainly seemed very pleased with her own joke.

Connor squeezed his arm around her shoulders, pulling her in a little closer. "You're a natural," he teased. He certainly didn't think any of his former girlfriends had ever progressed to the level of making hockey jokes. It was *nice*. Unexpected, but it made it easier to act as though they'd known each other for months.

"Come on, shall we take Banshee to the haunted house?" Connor suggested. "Seems appropriate." And, not that Connor felt he could say so in a crowd of fans, it *would* be nice to have a break. He couldn't help wondering if Ashley was the kind of girl who'd like being scared, whether perhaps she would cling to him a little bit.

"Alright, but you have to carry her," Ashley informed Connor handing the bear over to him. It was huge, but it did also look a lot smaller in Connor's arms than it had in Ashley's. Holding the bear meant that Connor couldn't also hold Ashley's hand, but they probably had done enough of that for someone to take a picture of.

When they got to the haunted house, Ashley led the way in, answering Connor's question about whether she'd be scared. "What are you afraid of?" Ashley asked. "I don't like heights, so I doubt they'll scare me here." It was a very confident proclamation, one which would probably come to bite Ashley in the ass.

"I'm not scared of anything," Connor answered, without even thinking. From the look Ashley gave him, it was clear she wasn't convinced. Connor paused to actually consider the question. As a hockey player, Connor wasn't used to *admitting* he was scared. That was an easy way to get shit from your team for at least a year.

As they pushed through the door, and the shuttered windows blocked out the light from outside, Connor found it easier to say, "I know it's stupid, but I don't like needles. Obviously, I have to let them take blood tests and shit. I'd never *voluntarily* go anywhere near someone wanting to stick a needle in me."

"Lots of people are scared of needles," Ashley offered with a smile. "One of my friends is afraid of dead chickens, including those rubber fake ones? So needles seem pretty sensible." That made Connor laugh and it was weirdly nice to have Ashley assure him it was *fine* rather than tease him about it.

They took a turn that led down a dark corridor. "I will scream if something jumps out at us," Ashley warned Connor.

"What happened to there being nothing here that would scare you?" Connor asked, amused by how quickly Ashley had changed her mind.

He didn't want her to feel bad, not when she'd been so sweet about his fear of needles, so he added, "It's a haunted house. I think they'll be offended if we *don't* scream."

Lights flickered on to either side of them, illuminating

a creepy-looking painting on one side, and a skeleton on the other. Connor had to hand it to them, it *was* spooky, and he moved away from the wall, his arm brushing Ashley's shoulder. "I'll protect you if anything jumps out," he promised.

"And who's going to protect you?" Ashley asked, and even in the dark Connor could see her raising an eyebrow at him. "Besides, I'm not scared. Just jumpy." And as if on cue, something *did* jump out at them - a zombie by the looks of it.

Ashley *did* scream, but only a small startled scream. "Ugh," she groaned as the zombie departed. "I didn't feel very protected." The accusation was definitely said in a joking tone, though Ashley did reach out to tug against Banshee. "I might have to carry her instead."

For a moment, Ashley's lack of faith in him did sting, before Connor reminded himself that she was only *pretending* to be his girlfriend. It didn't matter if she didn't think him brave and strong enough to defend her from whatever might be lurking. Still, Connor didn't let go of Banshee quite that easily.

"We can all protect each other," he insisted, trying to sound as light-hearted as Ashley had. "Maybe Banshee's actually the brave one. I bet *she's* not scared of heights *or* needles." In the dark, with no fans around them, there was no need for Connor to move closer, but he did, helping Ashley hold Banshee out ahead of them.

The next time they turned a corner, there was a flash of light bright enough for them to see the double-take as the actor in zombie make-up came face to face with a giant stuffed bear. Connor laughed so loudly, his shoulders heaving, that the actor had to shush them.

"I'm sorry," he muttered, between breaths. "I think maybe I ruined that experience. You want to get out of here?"

Ashley laughed, too, and it was a nice sound. "Yeah, we can go for lunch," she nodded before giving Connor a smile over the big bear. If Connor hadn't known better, he would've said that this felt like a real date.

◆ ◆ ◆

Connor had to hand it to Ashley, it took almost no time at all for pictures of the two of them sharing Banshee to hit twitter and, from there, the papers.

"What the fuck is *this*?" was his greeting as he walked into the locker room the next morning for training. "You've been holding out on us! And she's hot!" Glancing at the picture being waved in his face, Connor could only think that Ashley looked even better in person.

"I've been keeping it quiet," he said and didn't have to *act* sheepish. "You know, because of the whole -" He waved a hand at his arm, where he continued to wear a sticker over his soul-mark, despite it being an entirely pointless level of protection. Glancing around, it was Hayden's eye that Connor caught, and he almost winced at how somber the man looked. Given how private Hayden was about his own girlfriends, this was probably his worst nightmare.

"Is she *really* your soulmate?" Henry asked. "What's it like?" He had confessed once, after a few too many tequila shots, that his soulmate's name was so rare he'd literally never met anyone who used it. Connor couldn't imagine was *easy*, not if you actually believed in finding the one right person.

"It's... a lot," Connor answered, hoping the pause didn't sound like he was desperately trying to make something up. "I've met a lot of Ashleys, and she's met a lot of Connors, but I've never met anyone I *match* with before." Even with names as common as theirs, it *was* rare. "She wasn't hiding her mark," Connor explained. "So I knew before I even asked her out."

It was hard to imagine what Connor would've done, had he met Ashley under different circumstances. Ignored it? She'd made it clear that *she* didn't care for the idea of dating just because they had one another's names written on their bodies. Nor did Connor, not really.

"She knows nothing about hockey," Connor admitted. It would get it out of the way *and* teasing him about *that* would distract the team from asking more questions. "She's learning," he promised, "and she's coming to our next game."

"I hope you don't mean she's learning from *you*," Angie joked. "You need to get a *real* player to explain the rules." Everyone laughed, except Blake, who'd been oddly quiet since Connor had walked in.

"And *how* many penalties did you have to sit last season?" Connor quipped back, causing Angie to flip him off. "I've explained the basics, shown her a few games. She's catching on pretty quick." He smiled, remembering the kinds of questions Ashley had asked as he'd been talking her through it. "She's way too smart for me," he admitted. "She's doing a *Master's*." Everyone 'ooh'ed.

"Brains *and* beauty," Angie teased. "Are you sure it's *you* she's after, Lewis, and not someone more on her level?"

It made Connor briefly see red, and he scowled. It was fine when *he* said it, but he wouldn't have Angie making jokes like that, not about Ashley.

"Cut it out, McLeod!" Hayden was already calling across the room. "Her soulmark says Connor, right? Not Angus."

"Lucky thing, too," James joined in easily. "Imagine walking around with a name like *Angus* tattooed onto your body." Angie laughed, louder than any of them, and it broke the tension immediately.

"But come on, Connor, you've hardly told us anything about her," Henry urged. "The paper says you've been seeing her for months."

Put on the spot, Connor tried to think what he would've said about any previous girlfriend. Somehow, despite the fact they'd only met three times, he seemed to have a far harder time *choosing* what to say about Ashley. "Like I said, she's smart, she's funny. She gives me shit, but only when I deserve it." He coolly ignored whoever disguised an 'always' as a coughing fit.

"She's... different," Connor carried on, and the room

seemed to quieten. "She thinks about why people do things, so she *could* play games, but she doesn't. If she wants something, she just *tells me*." Connor felt quite sure Ashley *could* have communicated in hints and indirect ways. She would probably have succeeded far better than most of the women Connor had dated. It was nice that Ashley *didn't*. "I guess what I mean is, she's got integrity. She's not just a good girlfriend, she's a good *person*."

Whatever the response to that might've been, Coach interrupted it by shouting through the door to ask why the hell his team wasn't out on the ice where they belonged. In a rush of elbows and grunts, most of the players hurried off, leaving only Connor, who'd barely managed to get his skates on, and Hayden.

"I understand why you didn't tell anyone," Hayden said, giving Connor's arm a shove. He was rarely as boisterous as the rest of the team - except, perhaps, with James. "It's obvious you really like her."

Connor felt like someone had poured cold water over him - *again*, though this time in an unpleasant metaphorical flood. Connor had always thought of himself as honest, no-nonsense, and it was weird to discover he could *lie*, and lie well.

"Yeah," he agreed because it was too late to go back now. "Yeah, she's great."

CHAPTER FOUR

Ashley

By the time Connor's next game came around, they were well on their way to creating a PR story in which Ashley and Connor were soulmates. There were pictures of them together - the amusement park visit had done a great deal for that. Ashley had given Connor a list of talking points he could mention when someone asked about his soulmate. Things that didn't sound *too* committal but also wouldn't arouse any suspicion. It was... quite exciting actually to see someone use her PR suggestions.

Ashley hadn't really known what to expect from this 'pretend to be my girlfriend' thing, but she had to admit it wasn't... terrible. Connor was funny, kind of sweet and unexpectedly *nice*. More than once, Ashley caught herself with her mind drifting, often towards the shape of Connor's shoulder, or the way his arms looked in a tight t-shirt.

It was a dangerous game and Ashley stopped herself from having those thoughts whenever they occurred. This wasn't *real*. Connor was attractive, sure, but he wasn't interested in dating, at least not her. Nor was Ashley interested in dating *him*. Dating someone who matched her soulmark seemed like a stupid thing to do. People tended to assume they were right for each other and quickly stop *trying*. Ashley had little interest in that.

As it was, Ashley found it much easier to concentrate on their *pretending*. Part of that included her at the Howlers' home games. This wouldn't be the last time she'd have to come to a game, but as far as first experiences go, this was... oddly exciting.

Connor had done his best at explaining the rules to Ashley, and they hadn't seemed like very *hard* rules. Yet, Ashley was still constantly failing to spot exactly which player was Connor just because the game moved so *fast*. At least she *didn't* fail to spot when the Howlers scored. It almost surprised Ashley, the gusto with which she jumped up to cheer.

The Howlers won the game, which was good because Ashley and Connor hadn't actually talked about what they were going to do after the game if the team *lost*. Ashley might not have ever dated an athlete before, but she knew you didn't jinx a game with such talk.

Instead, they had agreed that Ashley would come out with the team. Honestly, she was a little nervous. Maybe even very nervous. She did remind herself that all she had to do was be Connor's girlfriend and it'd be fine. It seemed unlikely that the team would *quiz* her on her relationship with Connor, so mostly it was just the same sort of anxiety Ashley might've felt at meeting her actual boyfriend's friends.

As it turned out, she hadn't really had anything to worry about. The guys were nice, friendly, and very excited to meet Ashley. She was squeezed against Connor in one of the booths at the club, listening to the guys chirp each other. They were half-discussing the game, half-complaining about the calls of the ref. There was a strong sense of comradeship that Ashley found sweet.

She also didn't exactly *object* to having Connor's hard body against hers. Apart from the fact that he did make it quite *warm*.

Shifting in her seat, Ashley reached to pull off the hoodie she was wearing. When a sudden silence fell around the table, Ashley assumed it must've been because she was still wearing Connor's jersey, but the way the guys were staring at her arm quickly told her that wasn't it. Their eyes were focused on the way 'Connor' was splashed over her skin.

Never really bothering to cover her soulmark intentionally, Ashley was used to stares. She was just less used to them whilst her body was pressed into someone *called* Connor.

One of the guys - James, Ashley reminded herself - cleared his throat. "Connor said you wear your mark openly," he remarked and it didn't sound like a question but Ashley nodded anyway. "It's pretty rare. We don't even know each others' and we get naked together every day," he explained startling a laugh from Ashley.

She did also spot the way some of the guys glanced at Connor, clearly thinking how actually they *did* know his soulmark now. Not wanting Connor to dwell on that, Ashley bumped his chest with her shoulder.

"I was raised to not consider the soulmark something that defines me. My parents intentionally called me a common name, they're not soulmates." That, as it always did, earned a small gasp from somewhere, though most of the guys nodded. It was a lot more common these days for people to settle down with someone who didn't match their soulmark.

"But you still met Connor," someone else whose name Ashley couldn't remember pointed out and she shrugged.

There Ashley had to be careful because her first instinct was to point out how he wasn't even the first Connor with 'Ashley' on him she'd ever met. But they were soulmates, as far as Connor's team was concerned, so Ashley *couldn't* say that. She couldn't be dismissive of it even if her upbringing made her really want to.

Thankfully, Connor interjected first. "And I was so charming, she couldn't resist," he teased, making the rest of the team laugh and scoff, in roughly equal measure. As much as they teased each other, there was obvious affection there, in a way Ashley wasn't quite used to seeing with groups of all-guy friends.

"Are you going to wear yours openly now, Connor?" someone asked, even though Connor's t-shirt was *currently* short enough to show he was still wearing a sticker.

"I thought about it," Connor admitted, but he sounded like he wasn't entirely convinced by the prospect. "There's no *reason* to keep it covered, I know that, but I'm just so used to it, and the idea of letting *everyone* see…" He trailed off and then turned, unexpectedly, to Ashley. "Do you mind that? I never thought to ask."

"No," Ashley answered easily. Yeah, sure, people *did* stare, but because she had never bothered to cover her soulmark up, Ashley was quite used to people looking. Maybe if the name had been rarer or stranger, but 'Connor' was a fairly common name. It did sometimes lead people to approach her, telling her they were a Connor, or their son was, their brother, but that, too, Ashley was used to now.

"I think we, as a society, ascribe too much meaning to soulmarks," Ashley said truthfully. She wasn't terribly surprised to see some of the guys frown, unsure what she meant. "People hide them, so the soulmarks seem even more significant, secretive," she explained and someone gave a nod, which at least was reassuring.

"But everyone wants to meet 'the One'," another guy piped up and Ashley shrugged.

"That's one way to look at it. I think most people ascribe the label of 'the One' to people who match their soulmark just because they're so keen on meeting 'the One'." Ashley really didn't believe that such a thing existed, mostly it seemed that people just used that as an excuse to not bother more in a relationship.

The discussion was clearly not something the guys had expected, but at least a few of them seemed genuinely interested. Ashley was a little surprised by that. She'd kind of assumed that none of them would give much thought to soul-marks, but that was almost definitely her own prejudice about sports players.

"But don't you think it just *clicks* with the right person?" Nilssy asked, and Ashley did remember his name because he was the Captain - and as far as she was aware, one of the few people on the team who *had* met his soulmate.

Ashley had to tread there carefully. She realized that despite what she might want to say, what every part of her screamed at her to say, she'd just have to lie.

"Yeah," she said giving a smile before turning to press a kiss against Connor's cheek so she wouldn't have to say *more*. Except instead of his cheek, her lips landed against Connor's.

Ashley could *feel* Connor's intake of breath against her lips, the way he jerked his head almost to move back, and then seemed to reconsider. Her mouth felt like it *fit* somehow, against his, and the whistles of approval around them faded into nothing.

Connor's chest was warm and solid, and his arm around Ashley's shoulder tightened for a moment, pulling her even closer as his tongue brushed out in search of hers. She felt him move, jostled by Angus on his other side, but he didn't pull back.

Until, suddenly, he did, his blue eyes wide as they met hers.

For a moment Ashley seemed equally frozen. It couldn't have been *that* long because the people around them didn't seem to notice. The conversation changed to something that *wasn't* soulmates and soulmarks and for that Ashley was glad. She turned back, her shoulder still pressed against Connor's chest, heart racing.

Nowhere in their fake dating plan had kissing come up, but Ashley couldn't really deny that it had felt *nice*. Except, it was also *fake*, so it didn't matter if it was nice or not. Connor wasn't *actually* her boyfriend, and he certainly wasn't her soulmate.

The rest of their night out was mostly spent with Ashley

listening to hockey talk. Then she was told about all the dumb things Connor had done since he'd been on the team. And *then* she was told about all the dumb things that *everyone* had done since being on the team.

It was nice and the laughter almost distracted Ashley from the memory of how hot Connor's lips had felt against hers.

Ashley had been the one to suggest that they go home early. It was after some of the other - older - guys had already left. Ashley got the impression that if it wasn't for her suggestion, Connor would've stayed out and partied hard. He didn't seem to *mind* her suggestion, so Ashley didn't think she was robbing him of celebrating the team's win.

It had been her suggestion to go back to Connor's, mostly because Ashley kept thinking about their accidental kiss and how they probably needed to talk about that. As much as they had drawn some rules up - not literally, but they had discussed stuff - they hadn't quite talked about *this*. Not that Ashley had intended to kiss Connor but that didn't mean it couldn't happen *again*. Besides, she also wanted to assure him that she knew it had been an accident.

Like the first time she had been there, Ashley couldn't stop being amazed by the place. Connor's house was about three times bigger than the whole of Ashley's rented apartment, but then she did recognize that he earned a lot more money than her. It was easy enough to tell, though, that Connor had no sense of what went with what. The house was filled with badly mismatched furniture and not a single piece of art anywhere.

Ashley kicked her shoes off while Connor went to get them some bottles of water from the fridge. He threw one her way and she took a long sip before deciding what to say.

"So about that kiss..." Okay so maybe she hadn't decided what to say.

There was a pause, while Connor clearly waited for her to carry on. Realizing she wasn't going to, he made a noise in his throat, which wasn't *quite* a laugh, but sounded as if it might have started out that way.

"I'm sorry," he offered. "I didn't mean to put my lips in the way." He came closer, and Ashley could see a pink flush across his cheeks. "I would've -" He paused, hand opening and closing at his side like he was searching for the right words.

"Well, I would've *not* kissed you, except I realized everyone was watching," he finally said. How very *sure* he sounded would've seemed harsh, except that Connor *wasn't* her boyfriend.

It didn't make the hurt any *less*, though, Ashley realized. She did, she felt, a good job at not showing that. It still stung, how sure Connor sounded that he wouldn't have kissed her in other circumstances. Ashley knew, logically, that she had no right to be upset over that, they weren't dating, not really, but it still didn't feel *great*.

She let go of it, as much as she could, turning away so Connor couldn't see if there did happen to be any hurt flashing across her face. "No, of course not, I know that," Ashley said instead, walking over to the couch and taking a seat.

"It's good that we kissed, it makes it realistic, right?" She offered. "Your teammates definitely seemed convinced." Connor's teammates had been really nice and Ashley *almost* felt bad about lying to them. It wasn't like a terrible, awful lie. "Do you think tonight went well?" Ashley asked since Connor would know better if their charade was believable to his team.

"Right," Connor agreed quickly. "Couples kiss. We probably should've thought of it *before*, but better late than never, and no harm done." He gave a nod. "They've got no reason to question it, as far as I can see." He smiled, a warmer smile that almost made Ashley forget that Connor didn't want to be her boyfriend. "You've planned it all very well," he complimented.

"Well, I am a planner," Ashley shrugged, but it'd be a lie to say that there weren't at least a few butterflies in her stomach at the compliment. Ashley *liked* being a good planner and Connor's praise felt *good*.

Taking a seat next to her, Connor rolled his water bottle against his knee for a moment. "We never talked about whether you'd want your boyfriend to wear his soulmark openly," he said. "Especially a boyfriend whose soulmark is *your name.* Would it be weird for you for him to hide it?"

The question genuinely surprised Ashley. Not because of what it was, because it was a fair question, but because it was *Connor* asking it. She felt a bit guilty about not having given him credit to think of such complex issues, but the truth was, she really hadn't.

Ashley turned on the sofa, pulling her legs up, her socked-toes inches away from Connor's leg. "I wear my mark openly because that's what I've always done," Ashley said stretching her arm out against the back of the couch. Her soulmark was exposed with only the C slightly hiding under the sports jersey she was wearing.

"I'd want my boyfriend to do whatever feels comfortable for him." It was really the truth. Ashley personally felt that soulmarks were stupid and people ascribed them too much meaning, but she still knew that people *did*.

Noticing the way Connor's eyes were drawn to her soulmark, Ashley reached to pull her sleeve up from the C. "Do you want to touch it?" she offered, assuming that Connor had probably never touched anyone else's soulmark, especially not one that matched his name.

From the way Connor's gaze flew up to hers, it hadn't been something he'd expected her to offer. Ashley held her arm out, to show she was serious. Tentatively at first, Connor brushed a finger over the letters, his touch so light that Ashley giggled.

"I've only ever touched mom's," he said, answering a question Ashley hadn't asked. His finger moved to her hand, tracing the curve between her thumb and first finger. "It's right here," he explained. "So when we'd hold hands to cross the road when I was little, I'd always be touching it."

That was so oddly sweet, imagining tiny Connor holding his mom's hand. A shiver ran through Ashley at the touch, heat pooling low in her stomach.

He moved his finger back, moving slowly over each letter of his name. "Does it feel weird?" he asked.

"It tickles," Ashley offered with a laugh. "But it's not *unpleasant*," she added. It didn't even tickle because it was a soulmark and only because of how tender Connor's touch was. It made Ashley wonder what it'd feel like if he touched her *elsewhere* but she quickly got rid of that thought.

Slowly, so he could stop her, Ashley reached up to where she knew Connor's soulmark was. Ashley had Googled him, so the images had been hard to avoid, even if she'd been more drawn to Connor's naked chest in them than his soulmark.

"You can show me if you'd like?" Ashley offered.

Connor hesitated and Ashley could *see* the indecision written all over his face. It hadn't occurred to Ashley before to notice how open Connor seemed to be with his emotions. If it had, she'd have questioned whether he could convincingly *pretend* to have found his soulmate. He'd done alright in front of his team, though Ashley did recognize there had been a certain type of masculine bravado covering anything approaching *feelings*.

His fingers were still roving over Ashley's soulmark, but he slowly drew them back. After a moment, he moved to tug the sticker loose, revealing the neat letters of Ashley's name.

Even though Ashley had seen quite a few openly worn soulmarks in her life - most of her parents' friends didn't cover theirs - her breath still caught in her throat when she saw Connor's. Ashley wasn't even sure *why* because she *had* seen her name on someone else's body before, and yet...

She reached out to run her finger softly over the letters.

"It's smaller than yours," Connor observed. "But bigger than my mom's. She used to say that meant I'd find you earlier."

Her eyes widened at that, fingers stilling where they were brushing over Connor's skin. "Find your soulmate earlier, you mean," she corrected because *she* wasn't Connor's soulmate. Yes, Ashley had the same name as Connor's soulmark, but that hardly meant she *was* his soulmate. Of all the thousands of Ashleys and all the thousands of Connors just in this *state*, it seemed highly unlikely they'd be each others.

"Right," Connor agreed, pulling his arm away from Ashley's hand, his own fingers coming up to brush against the mark, as if he half-wished he could cover it up again. "She said the bigger your soulmark is, the longer you spend with your soulmate." The corners of Connor's mouth had gone hard, making him look almost fierce, and Ashley didn't think it was *her* he was annoyed with.

"It's rubbish, anyway," he continued. "If that were really true, someone would've proved it by now, done one of those studies about it." Studies on soulmarks did make the news relatively often, although their findings were usually so inconclusive as to be open to almost any interpretation.

Ashley felt *bad* for her words, but they were nonetheless what she believed. She also felt a little sad that she couldn't just promise Connor that the fairytales about soulmarks were *true*. Certainly not when Ashley herself thought it was all exaggerated bullshit. Yes, no one knew *why* people had soulmarks, but Ashley definitely thought ascribing too much meaning to them was unhealthy.

"Hey," Ashley said poking her toe against Connor's leg, wanting to distract him from whatever thoughts were going on in his head. "Bet I can beat you at *Mario Kart*," she told Connor with a grin, sure he'd take her bait.

Connor's head lifted, his hard expression vanished as he narrowed his eyes in mock-severity at Ashley. "Oh, you're on," he promised. "I am *undefeated* at the Mushroom Cup." It was startling how quickly Connor's mood seemed to change, how *easily* he let Ashley distract him onto happier topics.

Fetching the controllers, Connor handed one to Ashley before sitting down, his bare arm brushing against hers as he leaned close. "I'm so confident, I'll even let you pick your racer first."

◆ ◆ ◆

Obviously, Ashley had expected the fake dating to help Connor with his problem of having fans throw themselves at him as his soulmates. That was why she'd agreed to do it. One of the reasons, at least. It wasn't as if she wasn't getting anything out of it. Ashley had to admit she'd learned a lot about PR just from seeing how things had gone with Connor's soulmark being accidentally revealed.

What Ashley hadn't expected was how being in a relationship with a soulmate seemed to make Connor's public image *better*. It made sense, she knew that. People loved a soulmate match. Like she'd told him before, people loved looking up at celebrities and knowing they were living in some sort of fairytale.

Ashley just hadn't expected to be part of that fairytale.

There wasn't really much she could do other than to just accept it. In fact, what Ashley decided to do was more than accept it. While she and Connor hadn't agreed on a specific end-date to their fake relationship, Ashley knew it would end and that would probably impact on Connor's public image. This was what led her to decide she could make sure that didn't happen, or at least lessen the blow.

This was how they ended up at a charity event. It wasn't fancy like a gala - which was yet to come and Ashley *really* needed to figure out what one wore to a gala - and rather just a small event at a park. There were inflatable castles for the kids to bounce on, some high swings and a few trampolines. The main draw from what Ashley had read were multiple pie stands.

"So, I might've promised that you'll let some kids try to throw some pies at you for charity," Ashley said after she and Connor had been at the park for a little while. "I had to do something while you were signing all of the autographs for the kiddies." It hadn't exactly been hard to convince one of the pie sellers to let *Connor Lewis of the Madison Howlers* do something for charity with their pies.

Connor groaned, but he didn't actually look as if he minded the idea all that much. Ashley had seen how Connor was with the fans, how easily he became tongue-tied. At least for this, he wouldn't have to *talk*.

"And the press is going to just love photos of me covered in pie in the name of charity?" he asked, probably rhetorically, because *yes*, of course, the press was going to love it. "Aren't those stalls usually to throw pies at someone you *don't like*? A teacher or something?" he asked. "People like the Howlers."

"But people also like the opportunity to humiliate a celebrity," Ashley teased. "Besides, it's *kids*, you've just gotta hope their aim isn't very good." There was absolutely no doubt in Ashley's mind that there would be at least a few kids who would excel at the throwing, but that was hardly going to *motivate* Connor.

Reaching for Connor's hand, Ashley gave it a squeeze before dragging him over to where the pie stall was. The owner had even set up a seat and put up some balloons.

"It's great of you to offer to do this, Mr Lewis," the owner said, walking over to shake Connor's hand. "We're raising money for cancer research in kids, so it's a good cause." It *was* a good cause and it was good PR. Ashley didn't *say* that, because she knew it might seem cold. At the end of the day, everyone was a winner here. Especially the kid who'd manage to land a pie in the face of one of Howlers' star players.

"Thank Ashley," Connor suggested, slinging an arm around her shoulders to pull her more into the conversation. "She's the one who talked me into it." It was quite sweet, how he wanted to share the credit with her, especially as, in truth, Ashley hadn't really given him much of a *choice* in the matter.

"I do appreciate it," the owner said. "The kids are going to love it, and it'll save us having to worry about what we're going to do with all the pies we don't sell by the end of the day."

Letting go of Ashley, Connor settled into the seat, giving her a look as he asked, "Sure you don't want to come and sit with me, get some pies thrown at you, too?" They both knew *she* wasn't going to have the same appeal, not when he played for the Howlers.

"I'm good," Ashley assured with a laugh.

A line formed pretty fast, and Ashley somewhat easily fell into being the one to organize who got to go first and who got to go next. The first few attempts missed Connor by miles, but it wasn't before long that the first of the pies landed against his shoulder. By the time the stall was out of pies to sell for throwing (or eating), Connor was mostly covered in pie.

Ashley would've felt bad if she hadn't been so distracted by laughing. Not many, but a few pies had even successfully hit Connor's face, leaving smudges of strawberry jam in their wake. The owner of the stand had given Connor a towel but Ashley doubted that was really going to help very much.

When Connor walked up to her, he was still mostly covered in pie and Ashley was still mostly laughing. "You look delicious," she teased, reaching out to clean a piece of jam off Connor's cheekbone.

Connor laughed, leaning into Ashley's touch without hesitation. "You have to think that," he pointed out, "you're my *girlfriend*." He sounded so genuinely pleased about it, clearly unconcerned with being covered in jam and pastry.

"You looked pretty good out here," he added, "bossing all the little kids around. They loved you." A bunch of butterflies flickered in Ashley's stomach at that. She didn't *intend* for them to, but the way Connor smiled at her made it very hard to stop them. It was tempting to tiptoe a tiny bit more so she could kiss him, but Ashley didn't. This wasn't *real*, she reminded herself.

Lifting the towel, Connor made a half-hearted attempt to scrub the jam out of his eyebrow. "Are we going anywhere after this where I have to look presentable?" he asked. "If we are, I hope you're going to tell them whose fault it is that I've got a boysenberry stuck in my ear."

"There isn't berry in your *ear*," Ashley informed Connor. She did also take part of the towel to reach up and brush it over his ear just in case. "We're not going anywhere that doesn't have a shower, I don't want you to be *sticky* for the rest of the day," she added with a laugh. Ashley really hadn't planned for them to do anything but this. She did wonder if maybe she could suggest they watch a movie at Connor's or something. If that'd be *okay*.

Before she could, though, someone from behind her called 'Ashley!', making her turn around. "Payton!" She grinned, waving at her friend.

"I thought that was you," Payton said as she got to them. Her boyfriend, Edgar, gave Ashley a smile but his eyes then widened. He liked hockey, so Ashley could only assume that Edgar recognized Connor.

She didn't have to wonder for long when Edgar took a step forward, stretching his hand out towards Connor. "Hi! I'm a big fan, that was a great assist you did the last game," he praised and it kind of struck Ashley how *odd* this was. Kids asking for autographs seemed very different from someone Ashley *knew* telling Connor they were a fan.

At Payton's slightly confused look, Ashley shook her head. "Payton, Edgar, this is Connor Lewis," she introduced, though obviously, Edgar didn't need the introduction. "Payton and I lived next to each other in dorms," she told Connor.

Connor shook Payton's hand, smiling between her and Edgar. "Connor plays for the Howlers," Edgar explained, making Payton give an 'oh' of understanding while Connor laughed.

"I take it you're not as much of a fan?" he asked her, and Payton shook her head.

"It all seems a bit aggressive," she responded, with no apology in her tone. "Besides, Edgar has plenty of friends to watch hockey with." Connor looked thoughtful, but he made no attempt to argue that hockey *wasn't* aggressive.

"Were you studying PR as well?" Connor asked.

"Oh, no," Payton shook her head. "English Lit, much less... exciting?" There she gave Ashley a teasing grin, though, really,

Ashley *did* think English Lit was less exciting. "So..." Payton began and Ashley saw her eyes move down to Ashley's arm where the short sleeves of her shirt revealed her soulmark.

Edgar's eyes also fell on Ashley's arm but unlike Payton, Ashley doubted he'd *seen* her soulmark before. "Oh! Are you soulmates? That's great! Congratulations!" He wished in that way that people always did even though Ashley was very dubious all matches always *were* soulmates.

Connor grinned, though Ashley had known him long enough know to recognize that it was his for-the-camera smile. "Yeah, we met a few months ago," he confirmed. "We'd been kind of keeping it quiet because it was so new, but now we feel surer of each other, we're excited to talk about it."

Payton, who'd *heard* Ashley's opinion on soulmarks before, looked dubious. "Both of you are excited?" she asked.

"Of course," Connor agreed. "It's not something you really expect to just happen out of the blue, but when it does -" He shrugged one broad shoulder, which still happened to be stained with bright red jam. "It feels different than other relationships."

Ashley knew precisely why Payton's eyes widened at that. Payton had sat through *multiple* rants from Ashley about how soulmates just *didn't matter*, how their sheer existence was creating unhappy people. So to have someone tell her how *happy* Ashley was now that she'd found a soulmate was... not at all what Ashley was *like*.

Except she couldn't object, because objecting would mean blowing their whole fake-dating thing wide open. Ashley liked Payton but she wasn't sure she trusted her enough, and she certainly didn't know Edgar well enough to trust him. Not to mention that they were in a public place, anyone could overhear them.

So, Ashley realized, her heart sinking a little bit, she had no option but to go along with Connor's claims. "Yeah," was about as much as Ashley could muster but Payton didn't let it go.

"So *you* have found your soulmate?" She challenged and Ashley hesitated. She didn't want to say 'yes', but what choice did she really have?

"Yeah," she said, feeling almost cold at the lie. It had been easy so far, easy to lie to people Ashley *didn't* know, but she knew Payton.

"But you told Libby that she *couldn't* have met her soulmate just because her name matched Anton's." And, oh yeah, Ashley remembered that. Albeit, she had also been *right*, because Anton had *hit* Libby but somehow because she wore his name as a soulmark that didn't *matter as much*.

None of that was something Ashley felt like she could say, not without starting a scene and she knew *that* wouldn't look good for Connor. "Yes, well…" She didn't want to say she'd changed her mind, because she hadn't, but Ashley didn't know what she *could* say.

"It's not *just* that our names match," Connor waded in, perhaps sensing that the silence had stretched on long enough to become awkward. "We're compatible, too. I didn't just ask out the first Ashley I happened to meet."

"People do," Payton interrupted, and Connor frowned at her.

"People do," he agreed, his voice a touch louder than it needed to be, "but I didn't. I've met other Ashleys, but I didn't like any of them, so I didn't ask them out. I wouldn't have asked them out, even if I'd known they had my name as their soulmark. I asked Ashley out because she's funny, and she's smart, and she explains things in a way I understand, without making me feel stupid."

It was almost *painful* to listen to Connor tell Payton why he'd asked Ashley out. It sounded… real. Like he actually meant it, but Ashley *knew* that Connor hadn't really asked her out. What he had asked was for her to fake date him so the fans would leave him alone.

On top of that, having to defend how this *was* her soulmate when Ashley didn't really even *believe* in soulmates was…

it just all made Ashley's head hurt. "We need to get going before wasps find Connor and his jam-covered face," Ashley said jokingly, though there was an edge to her tone, not that she thought the others noticed.

"Yes, of course," Payton nodded and Edgar told Connor again how nice it was to meet him and how much he liked Connor's game.

"Nice to see you, we'll have to get a coffee soon," Ashley said before they finally could head towards the car. Ashley didn't really know *what* to say, thinking over the conversation. She hated that she had to lie but even more so than that, she hated how much she wanted what Connor had said to be *true*.

Connor didn't say anything either, not until they were a safe distance away. Glancing back to make sure they wouldn't be overheard, he turned to face Ashley. "Payton seems kind of rude," he noted, with an edge of irritation in his tone that surprised Ashley a little.

"She could've been happy for you, or something, instead of making it seem like you were doing something stupid just because you happened to be dating me." Connor huffed, clearly trying to vent some of his frustration before he added, "She doesn't even know anything about me, except that I play hockey."

Honestly, Ashley wasn't sure she could disagree that Payton had been rude. On the other hand, she did also know *why* Payton had been rude. "I mean, you could've maybe tried to sell the whole soulmate thing a bit *less*," Ashley said instead. She *knew* her tone sounded snappy, but it was easier to do this than to admit to herself how much at that moment she had *wanted* it to be kind of true.

"What are you talking about?" Connor asked, frowning. Ashley didn't doubt his confusion was genuine. "The soulmate thing is the *whole point*, why the fuck would I try to sell it less?" Connor's voice was never quiet, and they were talking loudly enough to attract a few looks. Connor didn't seem to have noticed.

"If I just wanted a girlfriend, I could've asked out anyone," he pointed out. "It *has* to be the soulmate thing, otherwise it's not going to work."

Somewhere at the back of Ashley's mind, she recalled someone saying that when you felt angry you should count to ten and then talk. That was as far as she got, because words were falling from her lips before Ashley had even finished that thought.

"Maybe because my friends might think it a bit weird that I'm suddenly so into soulmates?" She snapped, getting to the car and waiting for Connor to unlock it. It really wouldn't do to have this argument outside. At least Ashley could think of that much. The rest of her, though, felt *raging* with anger and it felt better than the *wanting*, so she stuck with that.

"Shouldn't you have thought of that *before*?" Connor snapped back, fumbling for the car keys. "I don't understand what you wanted me to say!" They were definitely attracting attention. As people around them stopped talking to listen, Connor finally seemed to register.

With a huff, he pulled the car door open, getting in and waiting for Ashley to join him before he picked up where he'd left off. "We can't pretend one thing to your friends and another thing to mine. That's stupid."

It made *sense* but that only seemed to annoy Ashley *more*. How *dare* he make her feel *sad* and then also make sense. It was highly rude and Ashley refused to stand for it. "And that's not what I'm saying. But you *know* I'm not... I don't..." Ashley wasn't sure what to say that accurately represented how she felt.

"It wouldn't hurt you to just fucking think before you speak," she finally snapped.

Whatever Connor's first response to that would've been, he clearly *did* think before he spoke. Ashley could *hear* the way his teeth clicked shut, and when she looked over, she could see a muscle working in his jaw.

The tension between them was palpable. Connor revved the engine and pulled the car out onto the road. He didn't say anything until they reached a junction, and he made the left turn that would carry them towards Ashley's place. "I'll drop you off at home," he said, not sounding like he was open to negotiation.

It kind of hurt Ashley that Connor didn't even want to talk about this, that he seemed to ignore how *she* felt. But she wasn't his girlfriend, right? So there was no reason Connor *should* care. That wasn't a nice realization to come to, but it was *true*.

"Okay," was all Ashley offered before they fell into an uncomfortable silence. By the time they reached Ashley's she no longer *wanted* to talk, feeling so annoyed at Connor and at the situation as a whole. And at herself. Truth was, Ashley felt angry at herself for getting angry. This wasn't their agreement.

Ashley couldn't even bring herself to say anything. Before Connor could, she was already slamming the car door shut behind her. Whatever he'd say right now would only irritate her anyway and Ashley just didn't want to *fight*.

Without looking back she walked into her apartment building.

CHAPTER FIVE

Connor

Connor had spent half the evening slouched in his apartment, waiting for a call to let him know that Ashley had backed out of their agreement. He had known she didn't think soulmates were *important*, he just hadn't realized how vehemently she was against the idea of having one. Or *pretending* to have one. Ashley wasn't his soulmate, any more than he was hers. That much was perfectly obvious.

It wasn't until he collapsed onto his bed, wondering why the call hadn't come, that Connor really did stop to think about what he'd said. He *had* known that Ashley didn't believe in soulmates. She'd said none of her friends would find it odd that she had a new boyfriend, but she definitely hadn't said that they'd be excited by the idea of her finding her soulmate. Connor had just assumed they would because *everyone* was excited about soulmates.

Everyone but Ashley.

It wasn't as if Connor believed Ashley *was* his soulmate. He had never been looking for that. He still wasn't. He'd dated plenty of girls with other names, been *serious* with girls who weren't his soulmate. At least, as serious as he could be, at twentysomething and knowing his next several years were going to prioritize hockey over romance. He just also knew how excited his mom would be, if he found a *nice* Ashley to go out with. She would hope for him, no matter how he tried to convince her not to.

It all made Connor's head hurt. He was grateful to be able to close his eyes and stop thinking about it.

After practice the next day, Connor still hadn't heard from Ashley. The newspapers had splashed his pie-covered face over the sports section. Fortunately, they'd been too full of his charitable actions to cover the fight. Connor found himself missing what Ashley would've had to say about it all.

She hadn't resigned. Connor had to believe that if she were *seriously* so pissed she couldn't stand the sight of him, she would've done so. That being the case, he drove over to her apartment after training, carrying the newspapers under one arm.

His stomach flipped nervously as he listened to her footsteps approach the door. "Hi," he offered, quietly, not quite sure what he was letting himself in for. "Can I come in?"

She didn't say anything at first but Ashley did also take a step back. Connor took the way she held the door open to be an invitation. Closing the door behind them, Ashley led Connor through to the living room. Her flat was much smaller than his house, but it was decorated in a way that made it feel quite *homely*.

"Do you want a drink?" Ashley asked. Connor had to wonder if it was more because she was a good host than because she wanted to give him a drink.

"Maybe in a minute," Connor answered. If Ashey was still mad at him, he didn't want to have to hang around while he finished a drink before he could leave. On the other hand, he didn't want to say *no*. That just sounded rude.

They stood, neither of them saying anything until Connor finally sighed. "I'm sorry about yesterday," he said, slowly. "You were right, I didn't think." It pained him. Not because Connor particularly needed to be right all the time, but because he didn't want Ashley to think he was stupid. He knew he wasn't as smart as she was, but actually admitting that he'd been an idiot made him feel like she *must* look down on him.

"I knew that you don't care about soulmates, and I didn't think about the fact your friends would know that." Connor still wasn't sure what he *should* have said, but he could at least have shut up. "If you want to tell your friends one thing and the press another, we can make that work."

There was a small hesitation before Ashley spoke. Connor was surprised when the first thing she said was, "I'm sorry, too." There was a genuineness in her tone, almost a sadness that was difficult to place. When she spoke again, it seemed to have cleared a bit.

"It's not... I don't..." There Ashely paused. Shaking her head, she sat down on the sofa, like she needed the support it offered. She patted the space next to her so Connor would sit down, too, before turning on the sofa to look at him. It reminded him of the way they'd sat when Ashley had offered to let him touch her soulmark.

"I know what our agreement is, I know that you asked me to be your fake soulmate not just your fake girlfriend," she said slowly. "Yes, we needed Payton and Edgar not to suspect we're not. I was just... if I didn't want to blow it, I had to go with what you were saying and what you were saying was... I don't..." It was difficult to really follow *what* she was trying to say.

"It was too much?" Connor guessed. "Too much about you being *excited* about finding a soulmate, I mean." He paused because it *hurt* to think that Ashley wouldn't be excited. That was stupid. Connor was *not* her soulmate, but even if he were, that didn't mean they should spend their whole lives together. Why would he expect Ashley to be excited?

Shaking his head, Connor tried to find something else to say. "I don't know," he admitted, once again feeling a sinking sensation in his stomach. Maybe he *was* too stupid to know how to handle a situation like this. If so, there was no use trying to hide it, as much as Connor might've preferred not to admit ignorance. "I don't know how we convince people we *are* soulmates without also making it seem like we're happy about it."

"Connor, people automatically assume that if two people with matching soulmarks are dating they're soulmates," Ashley told him. "Even if it doesn't work out in the end, plenty of people *still* assume you were soulmates. We live in a society that insists soulmates must meet, must get together. *No one* will question us being soulmates."

She paused there, and Connor could only assume it was so he could think about what she said.

And Connor did *try* to think. It wasn't particularly easy, not with the way Ashley was just looking at him. Connor couldn't help imagining she was waiting impatiently for him to *get* it. He didn't want to keep her waiting, but Connor's thoughts were slow to get themselves into any kind of logical order.

"Okay," he said, mostly because he *had* to break the silence, "but Edgar did ask *if* we were soulmates. And you don't want me to say that we don't know yet, because that doesn't fit with what we're telling the team and everyone in the press. Do you want *me* to act like I don't think soulmates matter, either?" Connor wasn't sure he *did* think soulmates mattered, but that wasn't what he'd told his team. It was complicated enough to tell *one* lie, let alone two different ones.

"No, sorry, I guess I didn't explain that well," Ashley said, shaking her head. "What I mean is... you don't have to say we're *ever so happy*. People will assume we are. Everyone - most people at least - will assume that if you think someone's your soulmate you're happy." That, at least, Connor did get. He'd seen enough people who had found their soulmate and were... probably happy.

Reaching out slowly, Ashley brushed her fingers over Connor's hand, startling him a little. He didn't pull away. "Just say we're soulmates, people will fill all the gaps themselves."

It seemed simple enough, and yet Connor still felt like there was something missing. If he were really dating Ashley, he *would* have been happy, and he would have told people he was happy. Especially Ashley's friends. He didn't want to annoy Ashley by asking what he was supposed to do *if* someone asked - as Payton had done - whether they were excited. He also didn't want to risk sounding any more stupid than he already had.

He turned his hand over, catching Ashley's fingers briefly to squeeze them. "I'll try to leave some gaps, in future, for people to fill," he offered. He wasn't sure if that was *enough*, or if there was still more. "Do you want me to explain to Payton?"

"I don't," Ashley shook her head straight away. "It's fine just... don't speak for me, okay? If you want to say *you* are excited, that's cool, be excited. Don't tell people how *I* feel." Despite the way she sounded frustrated - maybe more at the situation than at him, Connor hoped - Ashley didn't withdraw her fingers from Connor's hand.

It did make sense, and it occurred to Connor that speaking for his girlfriends was something he'd done before. He'd never thought of it as a *problem*. He hoped it *hadn't* been, but he could see why he should at least have considered it. "I'm sorry," he offered, and this time he really meant it. It wasn't just something to say because he wanted to smooth things over.

He couldn't quite meet Ashley's eyes, but he didn't let go of her fingers. He'd only intended to hold them for a moment. It still hurt, that Ashey wasn't excited, didn't even want to *pretend* to be excited. Connor could respect that it was her business. She was already going along with his wishes by pretending to be his soulmate at all.

"You know you can back out, right?" he asked, the words surprising even him. "If it's making you uncomfortable. I wouldn't be annoyed."

There was a pause and Connor could almost *see* her thinking about it. It made him feel unexpectedly anxious, not knowing what she might decide and risking that what she did decide was to no longer be Connor's fake soulmate.

"I don't want to back out," Ashley said and Connor almost gave an audible sigh of relief. "Did you mean what you said?

About how you... like being around me because I'm funny and smart? Because I explain things and don't make you feel stupid?"

The question surprised him, and Connor did look up at Ashley then. "Of course I meant it," he answered. He wasn't *smart* enough to tell a lie that convincing, he was sure. He didn't say *that*. "You explained this without making me feel stupid," Connor added, gesturing between them. Connor *had* felt his lack of intelligence, but it wasn't because of anything Ashley had said.

"You explained not to speak for you. None of my other girlfriends have ever said that." He gave Ashley a look, one that meant to communicate he doubted it was because they hadn't ever *felt* as Ashley felt.

"Well, maybe you should've tried a fake girlfriend before," she teased, giving Connor a grin. The way she smiled made him want to smile back. "It's nice," Ashley added after a moment, sounding more serious.

"It's nice that I can make you feel like that." There was a definite genuineness in her tone and it made Connor's stomach flip. "I don't think you're stupid, and clarifying things is hardly a challenge." There she paused. "Normally," Ashley corrected. "I'm sorry for being snappy with you yesterday."

"Maybe it's not a challenge to *you*," Connor said, with a shrug. He had definitely met people who made him feel stupid. He was quite sure, even from as little as he'd seen of her, that Payton would've been one of them. Ashley was different, she made Connor *feel* different -

And those weren't thoughts Connor could let himself have. He'd already risked ruining this charade once by being thoughtless. He couldn't risk it again by letting his feelings run away with him. Ashley was smart and funny, and she made Connor feel good, most of the time, but only as a *friend*, and a fake soulmate.

"What have your other boyfriends been like?" Connor asked. He had a feeling the answer wasn't going to be 'hockey players'.

Ashley seemed a little surprised by his question but if she didn't want to answer it, it didn't show. "Liberal, political," she shrugged. "I've never dated a professional athlete," she said with a grin. "But then I've never fake-dated anyone at all." Because yeah, Connor wasn't *actually* her boyfriend. That was something he had to remind himself of.

"None of them really thought I was funny or good at explaining things. And all of them thought I was too bossy." There was almost a sort of sadness in her tone at that before Ashley shook her head. "I guess some people just hate planning," she joked.

Connor wanted to say that Ashley's boyfriends sounded like worse idiots than he was if they hadn't appreciated her planning things for them. He worried how it would make him sound. *He* wasn't political, what right did he have to say they sounded stupid?

"Guess I'm just lazy," he teased back, finding that far more comfortable. "I'm happy to let you do all the work in this fake-relationship." He grinned. It wasn't true that he expected Ashley to do *all* the work, but he was happy to keep letting her plan their dates - and their media strategy.

"I don't really know *what* my girlfriends thought of me," Connor admitted, with a frown. "Mostly they just didn't want to come second to hockey." Connor couldn't really blame them for that. It was something plenty of his teammates struggled with as well. "Nilssy's about the only one of us who manages to have a girlfriend *and* a career," he said, with a shrug.

"Maybe I just get it more because I also want to make a career for myself," Ashley said. "You know how I mentioned the job in Dallas? It's a great opportunity for me, so I totally get how important your job is to you." And perhaps hockey wasn't quite the same as PR, but Connor *could* understand the wish to do well in his profession. It did, however, also remind him that Ashley would leave in a few months' time.

"What's the job?" he asked. He didn't really know how PR

worked, at least not outside of hockey. "Will you specialize in a certain kind of celebrity? I assume it's a bit different working with the sports reporters than the more mainstream ones." Connor *did* know that sports journalists tended to work exclusively on sports for their whole career. In some cases, they never wrote about anything except their sport of choice.

Ashley laughed at his observation but did also nod. "It's a bit different," she agreed. "There are similarities. I don't want to specialize in working with celebrities, I want to work with brands." That did seem different than working with a celebrity, but again, Connor didn't really know much about it to judge.

"What about you? Did you ever think about how you might do anything but hockey or was it always going to be this? The NHL? That's a huge achievement, right?"

Connor beamed. It *was* a huge achievement, and he was proud to have made it, prouder still that he was on a team as good and as successful as the Howlers. "I'd have given up anything to play hockey," he said. "I know that isn't always enough, but I got lucky." Connor had friends who hadn't been so fortunate, and it wasn't because they'd wanted it any less than he had, or trained any less hard.

"You're more than just lucky," Ashley pointed out. At Connor's confused look she shrugged. "I read up on you, the sports journalists are very flattering about your gameplay." It seemed somehow *sweet* that Ashley had done that, even if it was probably only for PR reasons.

Realizing he was still holding Ashley's hand, Connor slowly let go, rubbing his fingers awkwardly against the denim of his pants. "I never counted on it, not until the ink dried on the contract. Mom always said I would do well, but -" The silence stretched on as Ashley gave him time to consider whether he wanted to keep talking. "She's very optimistic," he finally settled on. "And I love her, but sometimes... it's a bit much."

"A bit much because she's so optimistic?" Ashley asked. It was clear that she was a little confused by what Connor meant. From the very little they'd spoken about Ashley's family, Connor got the impression that her parents were somewhat different from his own.

Connor nodded, taking the time to try to find the right words to explain. "She's not always... realistic," he said, and then gave a chuckle. "She doesn't plan things - at least, she doesn't plan for anything going wrong."

It was, Connor felt sure, different from Ashley, who seemed very able to consider what might go wrong, and have an idea of how to deal with it. If the look on her face was any indication, Ashley found the concept of *not* planning terrifying.

"When it came to hockey, she was so sure I'd get signed, she didn't ever think it worth me making a back-up plan." Feeling he was doing his mom an injustice, Connor hurried on, "I love that. Now that I *have* signed, she couldn't be more supportive if she tried. When it was all still uncertain, I didn't really feel I could talk to her about what I'd do if I couldn't make it in hockey."

Ashley nodded as if she understood what Connor meant and it felt... it felt like she did. There was just something about being able to *tell* her this, so easily and openly. "It's definitely sweet that she believes in you so much," Ashley nodded. "And it seems like she's right to, too." Her tone was slightly more teasing there, but somehow Connor also didn't doubt that she *meant it*.

"What about your dad? Is he as supportive?" Ashley asked.

Connor snorted a laugh, unable to help it at the idea of his dad being *supportive.* His dad barely seemed to follow what his kids were up to. "No," Connor answered decidedly, and then wished he hadn't. He didn't talk about his dad much. He had nothing positive to say, but it didn't feel *fair* to talk badly of him.

"It was from him I learned not to assume everything would work out how I wanted," he offered. That was giving Alex Lewis too much credit, but Connor would rather that than give him too little. "Not that he had much interest in back-up plans, but he didn't just assume the best, either."

Preferring to talk about almost anything else, Connor cast back into the conversation. "Why brands, rather than celebrities?" he asked. He was positive Ashley would've thought about it and would have a reason - even if it wasn't necessarily a reason Connor could understand without explanation.

If Ashley noticed the way Connor changed the conversation - and she probably did because Connor had learned that she was very perceptive - she didn't comment on it. Instead, Ashley just shifted to get more comfortable on the sofa and then answered Connor's question.

"Celebrities are just brands," Ashley pointed out. At Connor's frown, she proceeded to explain. "It's all about how you sell something. I find it fascinating how all decisions are prethought. How things are marketed is a lot about knowing your audience. Brands appeal to a wider subsection. So like... more different people need to like it, you know? Celebrities have more of a narrow audience."

While it definitely wasn't something that Connor had ever thought about, he enjoyed listening to Ashley. She just looked so *animated*, her whole body seeming to light up from the inside. It was, Connor thought, the same way a lot of the team looked when they talked about hockey. With them, Connor didn't find it *sexy*, and on Ashley he really was.

"So is a narrow audience easier, or harder?" he asked. He couldn't quite tell from Ashley's description. It seemed like it could go either way. He did smirk slightly, and add, "If I were a betting man, I'd say a broader audience is harder. I have a feeling you want your work to challenge you."

"Yes," Ashley nodded and there was just a touch of blush in her cheeks which somehow made her look *even* sexier. "Broader audiences can be harder because you still need to divide it and find core values that are similar," she explained.

She gave Connor a grin then. "This is... nice. I wouldn't really have expected you to..." Whatever was going to follow that, Ashley paused. "Be interested," she finished. Connor didn't know if that was what she originally was going to say but it still seemed like a *good* thing.

It made Connor wonder who, in Ashley's life, *hadn't* been interested. He felt almost annoyed with whoever it had been. He didn't say so. He worried it would count as speaking for - or feeling for - Ashley. Besides, as her fake-boyfriend, he wasn't sure it was his place. "It's interesting," he said, with a small shrug. "I don't know if I really *understand* it." It was unlikely Connor would, without a degree in it, but equally unlikely that he needed to.

"Are your parents supportive?" he asked, hoping it wasn't a question Ashley would prefer not to answer. "I know it can be hard on parents when they've got kids who need to move around for work." Naturally, most of the men Connor had played with, or played against, had parents who lived hours and hours from where their children were working.

"Oh yeah, my parents are great," Ashley said with a wide smile. It was evident that she loved her parents a lot. "They wish I wanted to do something slightly less corporate, but they also want me to do stuff that would excite me." Ashley defin-itely had mentioned how liberally-minded they were. Connor took that to mean they were a bit hippy-ish, so not wanting their daughter to work for a corporation made sense.

It struck Connor that he'd never get to meet them to see for himself just how liberal they were. The thought left his chest feeling strangely hollow, and it took him a moment to realize Ashley was waiting for him to say more. "Sorry," he said, giving her an easy smile. "I just realized how much of your time I've taken up." He really had only intended to stop by to apologize, maybe hash their disagreement out. He hadn't expected it to turn into a long conversation.

"I should probably get going," he said. He thought Ashley looked a little disappointed, but surely she must have her own life to be getting on with? She hadn't *planned* to spend the day with him today. "I'm glad we sorted things out," he said, genu-inely pleased that Ashley was still going to be a feature in his life. For a little while, at least.

The disappointed look gave way to a soft smile and Ashley nodded. "Yeah, me too." She got up to walk Connor to the door. "You've got a game tomorrow, right? I'll make sure to be in the audience." There was something very nice at knowing she'd be there and Connor smiled at that.

"Good luck," Ashley said and before Connor left she tiptoed to press a kiss against his cheek.

Somehow, it really felt like it'd bring him luck.

◆ ◆ ◆

Ashley's kiss seemed to work. Not only did the Howlers' win the game, but Connor scored twice in quick succession. When Connor teasingly asked Ashley for a repeat before their next game, she agreed.

Connor wasn't counting, but there had since been *ten* good-luck kisses, not to mention a handful of good-luck phone calls when Connor had to be away for games. The Howlers' didn't always win, and Connor didn't always score, but neither of them had suggested that the kisses should *stop*.

Connor usually liked away games. He enjoyed getting out of Madison, even if it was only to see a different ice rink and maybe a bar, or a burger joint. This season, Connor found himself almost impatient to get home. He wished he could've swept Ashley away somewhere with him, just to hear what she'd have to say about the scenery or the game, but she had a job, and she had a final thesis to finish. Connor left her in peace, apart from spamming her phone with pictures of adverts that caught his eye.

The team teased him, pointing out how he'd never sent pictures to his girlfriends before. It must be a soulmate thing, they claimed, that Connor could miss Ashley so much, even when he was only gone for a few nights. Every time they said it, Connor felt as if they'd thrown cold water over him, because

Ashley *wasn't* his soulmate. Even if she had been, she wouldn't have wanted to be.

He was selfishly glad to be back, and to have the gala as a good enough excuse to keep Ashley from her work for one evening. It was lucky that he'd asked Ashley if she could dance because his own ability not to look like a fool on the dance floor relied on him having a competent partner. Ballroom dancing wasn't something Connor had ever realized hockey would require of him. No matter how many annual galas he attempted, he could never feel as graceful as he did on the ice.

Ashley had asked what she should wear. When Connor's answer to that had proved insufficient, she had told him to put her in touch with Nilssy's girlfriend. Connor had been grateful Ashley didn't expect him to go shopping with her. She'd sent a picture of her dress and, teasingly, told Connor not to wear anything that would clash. The instructions to pick her up at her house, with enough time to allow for traffic, had been a lot less playful.

The photo of the dress on the hanger had not, in any way, prepared Connor for how Ashley would look *in* it. The layer of sheer lace over some fabric that exactly matched Ashley's tan made it look almost as though she wasn't wearing anything more than some strategically scattered flowers. A neckline that dipped all the way to the band clinging to the curve of Ashley's waist left enough bare skin between her breasts that Connor could only think about putting his mouth there, sucking his marks into her skin.

Connor was still staring when Ashley came up to him, tiptoeing to brush a kiss against his cheek. Connor's hand settled immediately on her hip, and he wanted nothing more than to pull her close, and to lose himself in the scent of her skin and her hair.

"Wow," he managed to say when Ashley stepped back a pace. "You look amazing."

"Thank you," Ashley smiled. It did nothing to make Connor less attracted to her. She ran her hand over her side, but there wasn't any sort of shyness. She knew she looked great in the dress. There was something very attractive about that, too. "You look perfectly acceptable, I suppose," she added but there was a tone of teasing.

When Connor proceeded to just stand there - too distracted by Ashley - she gave him a small nudge with her shoulder. "So, are we going to this gala or just standing here all dressed up?"

Connor felt his face flush. He hoped he covered it by offering Ashley his arm. "Of course," he agreed. Helping her to the car, he held the door for her the way his mom had taught him before his first-ever formal dance.

Focusing on the road, Connor could *almost* forget just how good Ashley looked. He'd get a glimpse of her every so often, especially when she laughed, or when she updated him on how her thesis was going. She looked so *intense*, in a way that made her dress seem even more feminine and alluring.

Connor had been prepared for the photographers, and he smiled his best smile as he helped Ashley out of the car. "Ashley! Ashley!" The press crowded around them, and Connor was glad to have an arm around Ashley's waist. "Can we see your soulmark?" someone asked her. Connor tensed, resisting the urge to pull Ashley away. She could speak for herself. If *she* wanted them to hurry inside, Connor could make that happen.

"No," Ashley replied almost bluntly and it surprised Connor a little. She usually wore her soulmark so openly. It was only then, really, that he noticed the carefully placed sticker. "And you should know better than to ask," she pointed out. The journalist genuinely looked a little embarrassed at being called out on it. It wasn't *untrue*. It was exceptionally rude to ask, but plenty of journalists (and fans) still did.

When Ashley told him that they had posed for enough pictures, Connor led them inside. Ashley turned to say more to him about the soulmark. "They know it's there," she said, because yes, there were plenty of tabloid or fan pictures where you could make out Ashley's soulmark. "But I didn't want it to draw attention away from the cause tonight. Or from you."

Something about Ashley's voice made Connor feel warm, all the way to his core. She'd really thought about it, not just from the perspective of what would make good PR; she'd thought about *him*. Connor had to fight a sudden instinct to pull her into his arms and kiss her.

It took Connor a moment to remember that he couldn't, and another to remember *why*. "You didn't have to do that for me," he said, "but I appreciate that you did." Doing it for the cause, not wanting to overshadow what they were raising money for, that was easier to catch hold of.

"Shall we dance, then?" Connor asked. Despite his usual hesitance, he wanted to take Ashley out on the floor, and to watch the dress swirl around her as they moved.

Ashley gave him a small, suspicious look. For a moment Connor wondered if she actually would say 'no', but then Ashley nodded. "Yeah, yeah, let's dance," she agreed, giving Connor's hand a squeeze. "But don't step on my toes, okay?" It wasn't something he could promise for definite, but Connor could definitely promise to *try* not to.

Having Ashley in his arms felt wonderful, and as she'd promised, she moved easily across the dancefloor, leading Connor without letting it *look* like she was leading. Having her so close, his hand resting on warm skin left bare by the backless dress, also felt like a temptation Connor *couldn't* risk giving in to. Ashley was beautiful and lovely. Connor hoped they would stay friends, whenever the act between them had to end. He didn't want to ruin that.

He was relieved when Ashley brought them to a stop, sending Connor off to fetch them something to drink. Just relieved, he told himself, and not at all regretting that he'd probably never have a reason to dance with Ashley again after tonight.

CHAPTER SIX

Ashley

T he gala was like nothing Ashley had been to before. Sure, she'd been to some events that required nice dresses and good posture, but nothing like *this*. The charity gala that she was accompanying Connor to was *fancy*. The sort of fancy that Ashley hadn't even been too sure how to dress for. Thankfully, when Connor's advice had mostly been 'wear a dress', Ashley had been able to get in touch with one of the girlfriends of someone else in the team. Evie, Nilssy's girlfriend, had been precisely what Ashley had needed.

"Oh my God, is that the dress? It looks amazing!" Evie exclaimed the moment she spotted Ashley. Connor had gone off to get them some drinks, though Ashley suspected his real aim was to hang out with some of the other guys. She didn't mind, mostly because it gave her the opportunity to thank Evie properly for all the help the woman had shown Ashley.

"All the thanks go to you," Ashley replied with a laugh and Evie shook her head.

"No, no, I just made suggestions, you're the one who picked it and the one who wears it so well," she commented. Reaching out, she turned Ashley around so she could inspect the dress better. "You look *hot*!" Evie announced making Ashley laugh.

Turning back, she gave Evie's dress a look. "So do you." Evie looked *amazing*, the black dress hugging her in all the right ways. The compliment made Evie grin.

"Hugo certainly agreed," she nodded. It took Ashley a moment to remember that that was Nilssy's *name*. Hearing about the other guys on the team from Connor meant that Ashley forgot they had *real* names and not just the team nicknames. "What about Connor? Does he love it?"

That made Ashley almost instantly blush. Connor had definitely looked like he liked it. Her mind also helpfully supplied a reminder of the way Connor had brushed his fingers over her back, where the dress didn't cover it, sending shivers down Ashley's spine.

"I'll take that as a yes," Evie laughed.

"Oh, um, sorry. Yes. Connor liked the dress," Ashley said blushing even harder, which only made Evie laugh.

"Ah, young love," she teased. Even though Ashley *knew* that her relationship with Connor was fake, it was difficult to not let her stomach flip, to not let her cheeks redden more, like Evie's words were *true*. "How are things going?" Evie asked, drawing Ashley out of the thoughts circling inside her head.

She paused rather than answering straight away. Then a smile, quite by itself, settled against her lips. "Yeah, things are good. I think I've even learned hockey rules by now," she joked. It had been just under two months since she'd first met Connor, so Ashley had had plenty of time to learn. And she had seen numerous hockey games.

"Oh, God, yeah," Evie nodded. "When I first met Hugo and we realized we were soulmates, I thought he'd be so disappointed because I knew nothing about hockey. But now I'm like the biggest fan," she laughed, making Ashley smile.

"How long have you been together?" She asked curiously. Evie was lovely and from what Ashley had seen she and Nilssy were a good match. Even if Nilssy often seemed stoic in comparison to Evie's chattiness.

"It will be six years at Christmas." The smile that accompanied Evie's words was almost blinding. If Ashley had had any doubts about Evie's feelings for Nilssy (she hadn't), this would've convinced her the woman was completely in love.

Ashley honestly couldn't imagine being with someone for that long - and she was aware that six years wasn't *that* long. Her parents had been married for well over two decades and were just as happy now as Ashley remembered them ever being. The relationships Ashley had had, however, mostly dwindled out within a few months.

"Do you think it's different because you're soulmates?" Ashley asked in a way that she wouldn't have asked anyone who *truly* knew her feelings on soulmates. She was... curious. The pretense of being someone's soulmate had turned out to be a lot easier than Ashley had originally anticipated. A lot different, too.

Evie, to give her credit, did seem to pause to think about Ashley's question. It made Ashley like the other woman even more. Evie was sweet, friendly, chatty, but she was also *smart*. Ashley liked that she didn't just seem to jump onto the 'happy train' that so many people who had found their soulmates seemed to preach.

"I think it is different, yes," Evie nodded. "But it's still... we still have to work on things, you know? It's still a *relationship* so not everything always fits perfectly. We had more struggles at the beginning, but now we're... we're pretty good." There was that smile again that made Evie's whole face light up. It infectiously made Ashley smile, too.

"But it's worth it?" Ashley guessed.

"Oh, definitely," Evie laughed before her expression turned more serious. "Are you and Connor having problems?"

"No!" Ashley rushed to shake her head before she really had time to recognize what she was saying. When she *did* think about it, Ashley realized that it was... kind of true. She and Connor *didn't* have problems. They had had one argument and they'd sat down and talked about it. It was... actually pretty healthy. Apart from the whole fake dating and how they weren't really soulmates.

"Good," Evie nodded. "You've been very good for Connor. Not just because of the press, though I have heard that you've been making his public image *so* good that the other guys are getting jealous." It was definitely a joke if the way Evie winked at Ashley was any indication.

"Well, it's hard work," she joked back, making Evie laugh.

"No, but really. Connor looks... happier. Nilssy even said so and it has to be pretty obvious for *him* to notice something."

That made Ashley's stomach flip, butterflies fluttering inside it. Knowing that she might make Connor look happier, to a point where his *Captain* said so... it made Ashley feel good about herself in a way she really hadn't expected. It felt... *special*. She found it difficult to remind herself that this wasn't *real*. She and Connor *weren't* a real couple, it was all just pretend. Yet the butterflies in Ashley's stomach felt far from pretend.

"He's... different than I expected," Ashley admitted, realizing that it was *true*. Ashley hadn't really had a chance to speak to anyone but Connor about their relationship. It was different with him because they both accepted that this was fake, that it had a deadline on it, that they weren't *soulmates*.

"Oh?" Evie's raised eyebrow encouraged Ashley to continue, a smile playing on her lips.

"He's sweet and caring. I guess, I kind of expected him to be more... rebellious?"

"Ah," Evie nodded. "Yeah, that's you." That made Ashley frown and Evie laughed. "Connor's always been... maybe not quite a party animal. He certainly doesn't have the claim of sleeping around the most - that's James, in case you're into gossip," Evie winked at Ashley. "I don't think many people who don't know him really well would describe him as sweet or caring."

That seemed ridiculous to Ashley. She almost jumped to Connor's defense but Evie held her hand up to stop her, clearly anticipating it. "I'm not saying he's *not*, just that *you* are the reason he shows it." That... made sense, but also made Ashley feel *weird*.

"Anyway, I need to go find Hugo to make him dance with me. I swear that man hides from me at these things just so I won't force him to waltz," Evie announced with a laugh. Ashley was too distracted to really do much more than offer Evie a smile. "We'll chat later," the other woman promised before walking off to presumably find her boyfriend.

The conversation left Ashley feeling confused. Obviously, Evie didn't know that her dating Connor was fake, but even so, her words had felt so *nice*. Ashley realized that she *wanted* that, she wanted to be the reason Connor looked happier. And that was a very dangerous wish to have.

Connor had been pretty clear with Ashley that he was fake dating her because she was his fake soulmate. That's what he needed, not a fake girlfriend. And most certainly not a *real*, girlfriend, right? But it was hard to get rid of that idea circling around Ashley's mind.

Shaking her head, as if that might get rid of the thought, Ashley decided to go see if Connor, too, wanted to have another dance. And if, maybe, somewhere in the back of her mind, she hoped that his fingers would brush over her bare back again? Then so be it.

Honestly, Ashley hadn't expected Connor to be very *good* when it came to dancing. Nor had he really exceeded her expectations in that. What she had found unexpected was how much he let her lead the dance. One of Ashley's exes had been pretty annoyed at her the one time she'd tried to lead them in a dance (because he'd been *awful* at it), and Ashley had somewhat expected that reaction again. Connor didn't react badly. If anything, he seemed to enjoy that she led since it meant most of his mistakes went unnoticed.

It was also very easy to just forget everything else around them as the two of them spun circles on the dance floor. Connor's hand - as Ashley had hoped - was neatly settled against her lower back, fingers soft against her skin. They felt *hot* in the most pleasurable of ways. Ashley kept accidentally forgetting how much she shouldn't be enjoying it.

"May I interrupt?" Someone asked tapping on Connor's shoulder just as the song finished. Ashley was a little surprised to find that she hadn't even realized it was nearing the end, so absorbed in being close to Connor.

Connor gave the interrupter - Blake, Ashley recognized - a suspicious look, but there was a playfulness in that, too. He looked at Ashley, and she realized it was to see if *she* was okay with it. That somehow made her heart feel so much larger in her chest. She gave a soft nod and Connor looked back at Blake.

"I suppose," Connor drew out. "No funny business," he warned, making Ashley snort and Blake shake his head.

"I'll try to resist," he promised before taking Ashley's hand from Connor so he could lead them into the next dance as the music started. Blake was, Ashley realized, a great deal better at dancing than Connor. Yet, she couldn't help but feel a little disappointed at the loss of Connor's touch.

Blake spun Ashley round much more gently than Connor had. That was almost definitely because he just knew how to balance himself in a dance better. It was interesting and Ashley wondered if it helped with hockey. Then again, despite Connor's lack of grace in dancing, he was very good on the ice.

"I wanted to apologize to you," Blake said, making Ashley frown at him. Whatever she had expected him to say - not much, really - she hadn't expected *that*.

"Apologize? For what?"

As far as Ashley knew, there wasn't really anything that Blake owed her an apology *for*. The almost crestfallen look on his face definitely encouraged Ashley to hear him out. She waited patiently, watching as Blake clearly struggled to decide *how* to say whatever he wanted to say.

"It was my fault," he started with and really, that cleared nothing up. Blake seemed to realize as much from Ashley's confused look so he carried on, "It was my fault Connor's soulmark got exposed. I didn't do it intentionally, but it was still *my fault* and I'm really sorry, I know it... You had to go public because of that. Because of me."

Whatever Ashley had expected, not that she had really known *what* to expect, Blake apologizing to *her* for accidentally exposing Connor's soulmark really wasn't it. Blake seemed genuinely worried that she might be angry. While Ashley understood *why*, she really... wasn't.

"I know we don't know each other well," Ashley started, careful in what she chose to say. "But... I'm not really *into* the whole soulmate thing. I don't cover my soulmark," she did glance down at the sticker on her arm, "normally," Ashley clarified. "So yes, the media attention was probably not great and I don't think *Connor* would've chosen for the world to see his soulmark, but..."

Ashley paused, making sure Blake looked at her and gave him a small smile.

"Connor and I aren't together because we're soulmates." And wasn't that the truth. "We're together because we *like* each other. And part of that is being in public together. Yeah, you sped the process up, but it would've happened anyway."

It was surprising just how much that *didn't* feel like a lie. The only reason Ashley had *met* Connor was because of his soulmark being exposed. So in a way, she realized, if it hadn't been for Blake they might've never met at all. That somehow felt *wrong*, like a sharp ache.

"You're good together," Blake smiled and Ashley wondered if he'd talked to Evie. "He smiles a lot more now, it's kind of... well, weird really, but I guess also nice." That made Ashley laugh and she let Blake lead them into another spin. It was... exciting, she realized. Knowing that *she* was a reason Connor smiled.

As the song finished, Blake gave Ashley another look. "You sure you don't want me to apologize again?"

"Yes," she laughed. "I promise you, I'm not angry at you." Ashley really wasn't and truthfully, she doubted she would've been even if she'd been Connor's real girlfriend. Real soulmate. All of the feelings pressed forward, though, making her think about it so much more. *Want it more*, she thought.

With the song - and the apology - over, Ashley excused herself to go to the bathroom. Escape, really. As if hiding out in the bathroom was going to stop the sudden *need* she felt inside her.

Ashley hadn't expected all these comments about how *good* she was for Connor to affect her so much. And yet, she felt like she wanted *more*. She wanted other people to also think that she was good for Connor. And more than anything, Ashley realized, she wanted *Connor* to want her to be good for him.

Running a hand over her dress as if to straighten it, Ashley took a deep breath. She could do this. She could *not* get attached. They weren't soulmates, so...

Except Ashley didn't care about soulmates, right?

"Well, fuck."

Ashley didn't really have a *game plan* per se, but she had... a plan. Kind of. In comparison to the very detailed plans she'd normally have, this did almost feel like no plan at all, but she was still going with it. Most of it involved talking to Connor. Ashley needed to find out if... if maybe this could be something more than just fake, if Connor *wanted* it to be something more.

She'd found him talking to a couple of his teammates, asking if she could steal him away. They'd teased Connor, but Ashley had come to learn that it was a very important part of Connor's friendships with the guys. Neither attempted to stop Ashley from taking Connor's hand and pulling him with her, though.

"Do you think we could find somewhere quiet to talk?" Ashley asked, looking around.

Connor tensed briefly, but it didn't last long enough for Ashley to comment. Instead, she let Connor take her arm and lead her away from the crowds. "They've always got a room open," he told her. "In case one of us spills something down ourselves and needs to change a shirt." He gave Ashley a teasing sort of look. "It happens more than you'd think. Last year they served these fancy sliders with cheese cooked into the middle of them, it was a nightmare."

It took Connor a few tries before he located an open door which led into a sort of staging area. There were piles of napkins and tablecloths, but also a rack of suit jackets. "Is everything alright?" Connor asked once he'd closed the door behind them. "Do we need to go over strategy or something?"

Ashley almost laughed at that. *Strategy*. Yeah, sure, because that was what they did, right? They had a strategy. A *plan*. Except Ashley was about to fuck the whole plan up. Or well, she was seriously *strategizing* to fuck the whole plan up. It struck Ashley just how good Connor looked and he was so close to her now that she could smell his cologne.

"No," she shook her head. "Or I guess, maybe?" Because that was kind of why Ashley had gotten Connor in a *cupboard* with her. It was a big cupboard but it was still definitely a cupboard. As Ashley thought more and more about cupboards she realized she was most definitely procrastinating from *doing* something. Or even saying something.

"Everything's fine." Everything *was* fine. "I just wanted..." Ashley bit her lip because she wasn't actually sure she knew how to explain anything. So she decided to do something she felt Connor would understand better anyway.

With her hand against Connor's shirt, Ashley pulled him down, her lips crashing against his.

There was a moment where Ashley could *feel* Connor's surprise. She even worried that he might pull away, but then his hand was on Ashley's back, making her bare skin tingle. His mouth opened up to hers. Ashley found her body pulled tight against Connor's hard chest, his free hand coming to rest on her waist.

Connor made a noise in the back of his throat, a grunt of approval that seemed to send a heat all the way through Ashley's body. He pulled back, but only far enough that he could nip sharp teeth into her lower lip. When he kissed her again, he licked his way into her mouth.

It was everything and so much more than what Ashley had expected. His body felt like fire against her but in the most pleasurable of ways. Connor's mouth opened slightly and Ashley took it as an invitation for her tongue to lick its way into it. One of her hands came up to tangle in Connor's hair, pulling his head even more against her.

Ashley's other hand ran over Connor's side, bunching up his dress shirt in her fist so she could pull it higher. With easier access, Ashley moved her hand down so she could slide it under the shirt. Connor's hard stomach muscles twisted against Ashley's hand and *fuck*. He was *so hot* and Ashley wanted to touch *more* of him.

Connor groaned, letting go of Ashley for long enough for him to shrug out of his jacket. Then his hands were on her again. One big palm cupped her ass, hitching her against his body, where Ashley could feel his cock already beginning to stir. "Fuck," he growled, kissing his way down her neck, his stubble scratching lightly against Ashley's skin. "You look so fucking hot tonight," he muttered, between kisses.

His free hand moved up Ashley's body, his touch firm and solid until his fingers reached the bare strip of skin between Ashley's breasts. He teased her, touching slowly along the edges of her dress like he wasn't quite sure whether this was allowed.

It definitely *was*. Ashley gave a soft moan, hoping it'd show Connor as much. His fingers felt even hotter now than they had when they'd been dancing. Ashley almost couldn't believe it had taken her this long to get Connor alone in a... cupboard. They were still in a cupboard. Somehow, Ashley really couldn't bring herself to care. Even as the sounds from the gala flowed through the door, all Ashley wanted was for Connor to tell her more about how hot she was.

"You look really fucking hot, too," Ashley breathed, pulling against Connor with her hand that wasn't preoccupied with stroking over the six-pack under his shirt. She took a step back, dragging Connor with her until they hit the door. Then, using that as support, Ashley tilted her head back up to seek Connor's lips out once more.

He moaned into the kiss, the sound so low and deep that Ashley could almost *feel* it vibrate against his ribs. She wanted to do something to make Connor moan again, but could only gasp as his hand moved to hitch her thigh up, his cock pressing right against her center through all their layers of clothes. He felt *big*. Ashley couldn't help the way her body responded to just the thought of how he'd feel if they were skin-to-skin.

Connor evidently felt similar. He worked his hand under the front of Ashley's dress, his fingers stroking over her breast until he found her nipple. He tugged, lightly at first, and then harder in response to the noise Ashley made. He pulled away from the kiss, dropping his mouth to her neck, sucking hard enough that Ashley was sure there'd be a mark.

"Fuck," she breathed, nails scratching against Connor's side. She heard his breath hitch at that and it just made Ashley want to see how many *other* noises she could get out of him. Having Conner's hard body pressing her against the door made heat pool between Ashley's legs. She rocked against him, enjoying the sounds she got in response.

There was an almost desperate need in her that just wanted to feel *more* of him. Ashley also wanted more of this, the kissing and the rawness of it all. Having one leg around Connor's waist, Ashley used her free hand to pull herself up more. Connor helped her there, half-lifting her before he kissed her again. This was going so much better than whatever half-baked plan Ashley had thought of.

The skirt of Ashley's dress was caught between their bodies, and she could feel Connor fumbling with the material. If she hadn't been so preoccupied with the smooth skin of Connor's chest, she would've helped. She made an encouraging, almost *needy* noise when Connor's fingers found her bare thigh, stroking along the sensitive skin.

He had almost, *almost* reached the scrap of lace between Ashley's legs when he pulled back, his eyes wide and dark with desire. "Fuck." He didn't move, just stared at Ashley. She could almost see the effort of will it took him to let go and let her stand on her own two feet.

"What are we doing?" he asked as if it weren't very obvious what they'd been doing.

Ashley waited for a moment to see if he was *joking.* When Connor didn't say anything else she felt... awkward. The way he had suddenly drawn attention to them felt odd. Ashley also wasn't sure what there was to misunderstand when they were making out in a *cupboard.* It seemed less funny now that Connor was just staring at her.

"Kissing in a cupboard?" Ashley offered, but she sounded unsure. She certainly didn't *think* she'd done something Connor hadn't wanted. The kissing back, not to mention his hardness against her thigh, implied that he was interested.

Connor took another step away, leaving Ashley's body suddenly *cold*, and not just in a physical way. Her dress fell back into place. Connor's shirt was still untucked, his suit jacket still in a puddle on the floor.

"Yeah," Connor agreed and ran his tongue over his lower lip in a way that made Ashley want to follow it with her own. He looked almost as though he were going to kiss her again, but he stopped.

"We're not together!" he objected. "This isn't - it's not a relationship."

That... shit, did that *hurt.* Ashley felt it almost like a physical slap. No, of course, this wasn't a relationship. They were fake dating and that meant there was no making out in a cupboard. She felt so *stupid* to have thought that someone like Connor might want more with someone like her. He was a professional hockey player and no matter how nice a dress Ashley could put on, she was still a waitress Connor had asked for a favor.

"Yeah, of course, you're right, I'm sorry," Ashley said, managing not to sound like she was about to cry even if she felt like she might. But no! She wasn't going to cry just because Connor didn't want her. He had the right not to want her and they'd never agreed to do more than fake date.

This wasn't a relationship, Connor had been clear.

"I'm just going to…" The 'go' was replaced by Ashley waving her hand towards the general direction of the party. Before Connor could say more things to her that were hurtful but *true*, Ashley pulled the door open and let herself out.

She knew he wouldn't be able to follow her straight away, not with how disheveled he'd been. So Ashley took that as her opportunity to escape. To leave how embarrassing this was behind her.

It took her no time at all to call an Uber. If on her way out she pretended she didn't hear Evie calling after her, well that would just have to do. Ashley couldn't possibly face pretending to be Connor's girlfriend anymore tonight. She'd go home, pull herself together and then tomorrow they could go back to pretending. If Connor wanted that.

He definitely didn't want *her.* That didn't mean he'd break up with her. Fake break-up? Ashley didn't even know. All she knew was that she needed to get away and to stop feeling like Connor had broken her heart when all he'd really done was point out their agreement.

CHAPTER SEVEN

Connor

C onnor spent the rest of the gala in a daze. He tried looking for Ashley, sure she couldn't have just *left* without saying anything. When that hadn't worked, he'd tried calling, and when *that* hadn't worked, Evie had said she'd seen Ashley heading out and getting into a car.

It just didn't make *sense*, and Connor couldn't wrap his head around it. Things had been going well, or so Connor had thought. He'd enjoyed having Ashley around as his fake girlfriend - much more than he'd enjoyed having most of his real girlfriends around. He didn't want to ruin that, and anyway, Ashley was leaving in a few months.

Like most of the Howlers, Connor didn't have a problem with spending one night with a woman and then never seeing her again. Sometimes, that was what he wanted. It was a hell of a lot easier than trying to date, but it could never be one night with Ashley - they were... friends. At least, Connor hoped they were, and he didn't sleep around with his friends.

Connor didn't want a girlfriend. He couldn't prioritize any woman the way that she deserved, not when hockey had to come first. He'd seen what a man putting his work over his relationship did, had watched his dad put everything before his mom, before his *family*. Connor knew how it had affected everything around him, and Connor didn't want to be that person.

He'd wanted to ditch the gala and drive to Ashley's. Whether he wanted to talk or pick up where they'd left off, he couldn't seem to decide. He wished there was someone he could ask for advice from, but he quickly realized that the person he would've gone to for help understanding someone's motives was Ashley herself.

It would be best to put it off until the next day. Maybe by then, Connor would have forgotten the scorching heat of Ashley's skin under his fingertips.

◆ ◆ ◆

He hadn't. Connor's dreams had been an extended montage of exactly how good Ashley had felt, how hungrily she'd kissed him and how much he'd wanted nothing more than to tear her dress out of the way and cover her with kisses.

A cold shower had helped, but Connor's head still felt full of too many conflicting things. There was no training to focus his mind, because everyone was expected to be hungover, so Connor headed to the gym.

He pushed himself hard, setting three new personal bests and finishing with another cold shower. He'd hoped that if he ignored his phone for long enough, Ashley might call. But she hadn't, and Connor spent the evening losing at *Mario Kart*.

The next day, Ashley had arranged for them to go to a baseball game. She had said that it would look good for him to support Madison's other athletes. Connor had thought about calling, but he didn't want to hear that Ashley had changed her mind about joining him. Instead, he turned up at her place with just about enough time for them to drive over to the pitch.

He'd half expected her to still be in her dress because that's how he'd been picturing her since the gala. He didn't know whether to be disappointed or relieved that she was instead wearing a t-shirt and jeans. Even dressed casually, the curve of her waist made Connor ache to touch her again. *Fuck.*

"Hi."

"Hey," Ashley greeted and Connor was almost *startled.* Like somehow he hadn't expected her to just... act as if things were normal. He wasn't sure what he had expected but *something.* "I just need my bag," Ashley said making this somehow even more surreal. It didn't take her long to get her handbag and for them to start walking towards Connor's car. Glancing at her, Connor could see that unlike at the gala, Ashley hadn't bothered to cover her soulmark.

He was so distracted by her that Connor almost missed her question and had to pause to recall it. "I asked if you're the sort of guy who gets snacks at a baseball game," Ashley repeated clearly sensing that Connor hadn't been listening.

It felt weird to act as if nothing had happened. Connor wondered if he should say something. He didn't know *what,* and after all, didn't Connor *want* things to go back to the way they'd been before the gala? He enjoyed spending time with Ashley, he liked having a fake girlfriend to keep the fans and the press at a distance. Right now, it seemed like Ashley was offering to keep giving him those things.

"Is there any other sort of guy?" Connor asked, and though he tried to make it sound like a joke, it didn't quite work. It felt like there was a wall between them, something unspoken keeping them apart. It hurt to think that was how Ashley *wanted* it to be, and Connor found himself pulling back from their previous sort of chat.

"So, do I need to explain the rules of baseball, too?" he asked.

"Ha ha," Ashley said dryly as they got into the car. "I know the rules of baseball. All-American sport? Hockey seems more... niche," she announced and it took a moment for Connor to realize that she was *teasing.* When Ashley saw Connor get it, she gave him a wide grin. "Now, basketball, I don't understand at all."

"Really?" Connor asked, feeling as though he'd lost all ability to distinguish when Ashley was joking. "Basketball seems pretty simple - get the ball through the hoop and you score." It was *probably* more complicated than that. Connor had watched a few games with friends and following that much was enough to know who was winning if nothing else.

As he started the car, Connor glanced sideways at Ashley. He realized he was waiting for her to *say* something. To explain what had happened, because Connor sure as hell didn't understand it. He almost opened his mouth to ask, but any question he could think of just seemed stupid.

So, Connor did his best to take his cue from Ashley, putting the whole thing behind them. "You said you didn't grow up with hockey but were you into other sports?"

"My dad's a big fan of football and soccer," Ashley answered and it was almost bothersome just how *easily* she seemed to be having this conversation. "He's English, my dad, so he's always followed a particular soccer team. There's a lot of pictures of me in tiny soccer shirts as a baby," she laughed. It was *nice* to hear that, to hear her laughing.

"I'm guessing it was always hockey, hockey, hockey in your house?"

"Not at first," Connor answered, thinking back to his very first days discovering hockey. "Neither of my parents were really into it. Mom didn't care much about sports, and dad's always been a fan of college football. Maisy was the one who wanted to learn to skate, so mom took us both to lessons."

Connor had objected at first because there'd been no other boys in the class, but then he'd got out onto the ice, and he'd loved it. He opened his mouth to tell Ashley about the first time he'd seen a junior hockey game, and then stopped. Reporters weren't going to ask her about what Connor had been like as a kid, so what would be the point in her having information she didn't need?

"Mom's into hockey *now*," Connor finished. "She just needed a reason."

Ashley snorted, "Even *I'm* into hockey now." And that was... yeah. She definitely sounded like she meant it, too. And Connor *had* seen her at the games. Now that Ashley knew the rules, she cheered along. He was pretty sure he'd once even spotted her shouting at the ref from the stands like a true hockey fan. It was striking to realize that was because of *him*. Ashley had learned about hockey for him and supported hockey *because of him*.

"Do you think you'll keep watching it, after -" Connor faltered, surprised by just how much it hurt to think of this all being over. Ashley would move away, would probably forget all about Connor and hockey. He couldn't expect to have any *lasting* impact on her life.

It made Connor sad because he *wanted* Ashley to remember him. He knew he would remember her, and that thought frightened him. Every time he changed the sticker over his soulmark, he was going to think of Ashley. Every time he would wonder what she was doing. At least until he met *the* Ashley, but Connor had never really believed that would happen, nor wanted it to.

Desperately needing to redirect, Connor coughed, and said, "There're some okay teams in Texas."

Ashley didn't say anything for a moment and since Connor was driving he couldn't exactly look at her. Not for long enough to even attempt to figure out what she was thinking, anyway. So he waited. Finally, Ashley cleared her throat and Connor could see her give a nod.

"I think I will," she answered and Connor felt it was *true*. "I've come to like the coldness of the rink. It's... I don't know, it just feels good?" Ashley offered before shrugging slightly. "That probably sounds silly. Especially to you, I know you're at an ice rink like every day. It's just... it's new and I hadn't really expected to enjoy the games as much as I do, but, yeah."

Somehow, imagining Ashley at games *without* Connor was almost worse than imagining that she'd just forget hockey entirely. Connor could feel himself getting irritated at his own attitude. What was wrong with him? He and Ashley had made out, and it had been hot as hell, but that was no reason to let his head get all messed up. He had to focus.

He forced himself to smile, risking a glance at Ashley as they pulled up at a traffic light. "It doesn't sound silly," he promised, genuinely meaning the words. "I remember when I started skating. I felt like everything made sense at the rink, in a way it didn't anywhere else."

Now he was skating too close to topics he'd rather not discuss. Connor didn't talk about what his home life had been like then. About how he and Maisy had loved escaping to the rink because it meant they got time with just them and their mom. Their dad had never come to watch, he'd always had better things to do.

"Even when there's a fight, it feels... simple. You shout and you take whatever the other team has to give, and then you leave it on the ice."

"Yeah," Ashley nodded. The tone implied that there was more that she wanted to say about it but then she didn't. Connor wasn't very good at *guessing* what Ashley might be thinking but he also didn't know if he could ask. If she'd answer. If he even wanted to hear whatever the answer was. The awkwardness between them seemed to linger.

It was only once Connor started driving again that Ashley spoke up. "Do *you* know the rules of baseball?"

For a moment, Connor considered telling Ashley he needed the rules explained, just to give them something safe to talk about for the rest of the drive. In the end he decided that it felt weird to outright *lie* to her.

"I know the rules of Little League," Connor said honestly. "Is that basically the same?"

As it turned out, there were some differences, and Ashley was able to explain them. It struck Connor all over again, how nice it was that Ashley could tell him things he didn't know without making Connor feel bad for his ignorance. It almost made him want to ask her to explain that night at the gala.

Maybe if she could put her understanding into words, it would make Connor feel less *weird* about the whole thing.

Once they arrived at the stadium, they were greeted by a couple of sports photographers Connor recognized. All of them wanted pictures of 'the happy couple'. Putting his arm around Ashley's shoulders, Connor had to make a real effort not to *look* as uncomfortable as he felt.

◆ ◆ ◆

Connor was honestly *relieved* that he and the rest of the team were flying out the next day for a series of away games. Ashley dropped him off at the airport, pressing a kiss against his cheek 'for luck'. It left Connor wondering whether it would *still* be lucky.

He dozed most of the flight and felt so restless by the time they landed. To overcome it, Connor had invited Blake out for a run before they'd even arrived at their hotel. He knew running with someone else would push him harder, make him exhaust himself so he could actually focus on strategy in their pre-game meeting.

He and Blake raced through the quiet streets, trash-talking and urging one another on until they collapsed in a sweaty heap at their agreed finishing point. After each draining a bottle of water, Connor moved to get up, but Blake waved him off.

"What's up with you?" Blake asked, and before Connor could even open his mouth, his friend had carried on. "No, don't tell me it's nothing, you're a shit liar, Lewis."

That almost made Connor choke on a laugh, and Blake gave him a look like he wasn't going to accept 'no comment' as an answer. "Are you fighting with Ashley?" Blake asked.

"Why would you ask that?" Connor asked, hoping he could buy himself some time to come up with a plausible lie. If only Ashley could've been here, he had no doubt she would've known the right thing to say.

Blake shrugged. "You've hardly spoken since we got to the airport," Blake pointed out. "And you've been together, what, five months? About time you had your first fight." Connor blinked because he *knew* he'd only known Ashley for two months. It took him a moment to remember that they'd told everyone they'd already been dating for three before that.

"No," Connor said, not even sure what he was denying. "It's just - hard. Being away from her."

"Right," Blake said, and then just looked at Connor, waiting for him to go on.

"It makes me think, you know, that this isn't going to last," Connor muttered, and Blake's eyes narrowed at him.

"You're soulmates," he pointed out, "why would you think it's not going to last?"

Connor groaned. He knew soulmates didn't always work out, because his parents hadn't worked out, but it wasn't something he liked talking about.

"You're not doubting that she's the *right* Ashley, are you?" Blake asked. "Because if you are, I'm going to have to knock some sense into you." The threat, playful as it was, made Connor laugh, and almost instantly feel better, but Blake didn't wait for him to answer. "I know it's my fault, that you had to go public with her so soon," he muttered, and he looked so honestly guilty that Connor had to bite his lip to keep from revealing the truth. "So I consider it my responsibility to make sure you don't fuck it up," Blake finished.

"It might be too late," Connor admitted, feeling his lip twist. He didn't *want* to have fucked it up, but he worried that he was.

"You'll feel better if you just tell me about it," Blake promised. "Come on, you know I won't breathe a word." It was true. Connor trusted everyone on the team, but he was closest to Blake. They messed with each other, but for all that, Blake was probably Connor's closest friend. He took a breath, trying to find some *version* of the truth he could explain.

"Ashley's got a job offer in Dallas," Connor found himself

blurting out. "In a few months. She's taking it, obviously, it's a great opportunity, but -" Connor could feel frustration rising, frustration at himself, at the situation. "I don't want her to go," he admitted. "But if it were me, if it were an opportunity to sign somewhere, *I'd* go. I can't expect her to do differently."

"And that's what's got you all upset?" Blake asked, frowning. "Because you don't want it to hurt when she moves?" That wasn't all, of course, and Connor sighed, scrubbing a hand over his face. "Come on, you've got to have more faith than that," Blake urged. "You're -"

"*Don't!*" Connor interrupted his voice almost a shout. "Don't. We're *not* soulmates, okay? It's all a fucking con." His stomach twisted, and Connor didn't know if it was guilt at having lied to Blake, or guilt at betraying the truth now. "I found her the day the press published the pictures of my soulmark, and her name was Ashley, and *her* soulmark said Connor, so I asked if she'd *pretend* to be my girlfriend."

There was a silence between them, and Connor watched Blake's frown getting deeper and deeper. Shit, he had fucked this up so badly. "You won't - you're not going to tell anyone?" Connor asked, sounding small and uncertain.

"That's bullshit," Blake responded. "Ashley's not *pretending* to be your girlfriend." It was not the response Connor had expected, and he blinked.

"She is," he insisted. "She's doing her Master's in PR, that's why the publicity's been so good. It's just an act. She's not my girlfriend, and she's *definitely* not my soulmate. She doesn't even believe in them." And fuck, Connor hadn't meant to say that.

Blake's face was unreadable, and once again, Connor almost wished Ashley were there to help him handle this.

"Okay, putting aside that I don't believe for a minute *you* can fake a relationship," Blake said. "If it's all an act, I don't understand what the problem is. If she's not your girlfriend, why do you care if she's moving?"

It was a good question, and Connor didn't really have an answer. He liked Ashley, and the thought of her being miles and miles away was depressing. Connor didn't want to have to wonder if he'd ever see her again.

"I like her," Connor offered. "Not as a girlfriend, but -" It still didn't make sense. While it was true Connor didn't have a lot of friends who didn't live in Madison, he'd never not wanted someone to move before. If it was best for them, he'd always been happy on their behalf.

"And she likes you," Blake insisted. "Which is why I don't believe this story about it being fake. I talked to her at the gala. When I cut in to dance with her?" Connor remembered, and he gave a nod. "She definitely wasn't pretending," Blake continued. "I told her how good she was for you, and I promise you, Connor, she fucking *glowed* like it was the nicest thing anyone had ever said about her." Connor couldn't stop the smile that slowly spread over his face.

"Really?" The idea that Ashley had *liked* the thought of being good for him, it was oddly touching.

"And she *has* been good for you. Come on, do you really believe you were texting her all the time as some kind of ruse?"

Now that Blake mentioned it, it did seem odd. Why had Connor felt the need to carry on their relationship when it *wasn't* a matter for PR, or even for his team? He'd sent those messages to Ashley because he liked her, wanted to be in contact while he was away.

Shit.

"But she's still going to move," Connor pointed out. "And -" He stopped, uncertain. He'd already told Blake about the worst, though, about their fake relationship. What could it hurt to tell him the truth about the gala? "She kissed me," he admitted. "At the gala. Pulled me into a cupboard and -" Well, he wasn't going to give Blake *details*.

"And?" Blake asked, his eyes lighting up. "You're telling me she kissed you, but nothing else happened? What are you, stupid?"

Connor groaned because maybe he *was* stupid. "I told her we weren't together." Hearing it in his own voice now, Connor could *tell* how hurtful it must have been. Judging by Blake's wince, he could tell, too.

"I think maybe you need to talk to her," Blake suggested, giving Connor's arm a friendly shove. "But when you get back, yeah? Give yourself some time to think it through."

◆ ◆ ◆

It kind of stung, that even Connor's best friend thought he needed time to think something over, but Connor couldn't deny that Blake was right. Whenever he wasn't on the ice, he was thinking about Ashley, wondering what she was doing, and how she was feeling.

Connor had no idea if he'd messed it all up for good, but he was determined to find out. It was a determination which carried him all the way to Ashly's door, and then momentarily vanished, to be replaced by a host of anxious snakes writhing in Connor's stomach.

He hadn't warned Ashley he was coming, and he could see the surprise on her face when she answered the door. "Can we talk?" he asked. "I think I've been an idiot."

Having come straight from the airport, Connor hadn't really thought about what time it was, and it was only when he really took in what Ashley was wearing that he realized it probably was quite *late*. She had pajamas on but despite that, and the fact that she clearly was surprised to see him, Ashley nodded and took a step back to let Connor in.

Pulling her cardigan tighter around herself when Connor brought the breeze inside with him, Ashley shut the door, giving a nod so he'd come through to the living room with her. "Have you been an idiot about anything in particular?" She asked. "I watched your games, you did well," she added as if Connor was here to talk about his *games*. But then he did also have to stop himself from asking *more* about that. This was not about hockey.

"I was an idiot at the gala," Connor said, and days of preparation really had made it easier for him not to beat around the bush. "When I said that we weren't together, that it wasn't a relationship, I didn't mean it to come out the way it did." It had been *true*, but that wasn't the point.

"I didn't mean I don't *want* a relationship," Connor clarified, feeling his face heat slightly as Ashley's gaze moved sharply to him. "I just meant - well, that we shouldn't be making out in a cupboard without *talking* first."

The silence that then dragged between them was almost enough for Connor to consider bolting now that he'd said his bit, but he was a *professional hockey player*. So he could brave a bit of silence. Probably.

"So," Ashley began slowly and somehow that seemed *worse* than the silence. "I embarrassed myself by basically jumping your bones and putting myself out there, showing you that I *wanted* to kiss you, but you wanted for us to just... talk?" She didn't sound very *sure* of herself, which was not a tone Connor had really heard from her. Apart from when they'd been in the cupboard, just before she'd left.

"Talk *first*," Connor corrected quickly. "It's not that I didn't want you." Even now, he could remember exactly how fiercely he had wanted Ashley, how hard it had been to pull away from the heat of her body to ask what they were doing. "I *like* you," Connor offered, taking courage from Blake having assured him that Ashley liked him, too.

"And I don't want to sleep with you one time if that's going to mean we can't ever talk again, because I *like* talking to you," he carried on. If he didn't pause, maybe Ashley wouldn't be able to tell him that he'd got it all wrong. "I know I can't be a good boyfriend," he added, dropping his gaze. "Not right now, and maybe not for ages. I *have* to put hockey first, and that wouldn't be fair."

"So you're going to just decide for me?" Ashley asked with a frown.

Connor's first instinct was to object, say that of course

he hadn't wanted to decide *for* Ashley, but the truth was, that maybe he had, and if that was true, Ashley had a right to be annoyed.

Remembering what Blake had said, about Ashley glowing at the idea of her being good for him, was just about enough to keep Connor from backing out of this altogether.

"I know what it's like when someone's career is more important than you," he said honestly. When Ashley didn't immediately respond, but rather looked like she was waiting for him to continue, Connor sighed. "I know what it was like for me when my dad put his job first, and I saw what it was like for mom, too. Not that she'd ever admit it. It blows, knowing you're always second place, and I've never wanted to do that to anybody, but hockey is - Hockey's always been everything. I don't know how to have that *and* a relationship with somebody where I can make them feel important."

This time, Ashley took a step closer to him. It was slow and almost tentative, but when Connor didn't step back, she tiptoed and for a moment he thought she was going to kiss him again but Ashley didn't. Instead, she pulled Connor into a hug, wrapping her arms around him. It only took him a short moment before he hugged back, holding her body tightly against his.

"You've been a great boyfriend, Connor," Ashley told him. "Even as a fake boyfriend, you've been a *great* one." She did pull back then, the closeness of her face almost too distracting, but Connor focused to hear what she said.

Bringing a hand up to brush over Connor's cheek, Ashley gave him a small smile. "I'm scared, too, Connor."

Leaning into her touch, Connor still managed to raise an eyebrow. "You?" he asked, and though he'd meant to sound teasing, he could hear the note of surprise. "I figured you were fearless," he added, more sincerely. It was hard to imagine Ashley being afraid of anything, but it made Connor feel better to know that she was.

That seemed to startle a laugh from Ashley. "I only pretend for you," she said and her tone was teasing in a way that put some ease back into Connor.

"What are you scared of?" he asked, not because he couldn't imagine, but because he could think of so many different reasons to be afraid, and didn't know which of them were bothering Ashley.

The question made Ashley pause but Connor could tell it wasn't because she didn't want to answer it. Taking a step back, Ashley reached to take Connor's hand, giving it a small squeeze. She led them over to the couch, but Connor was glad when she didn't let go of his hand.

"I'm scared because I've never felt like this. I like being around you, I *want* to be around you. I'm scared that you don't, or that you don't want to. But I want to... I want to *try*."

It made Connor feel as though his heart gave a wild leap in his chest, and he grinned, suddenly unafraid of looking like an idiot. "I *do* want to be around you," he assured. "I think about you all the time when you're not there. About what you'd say, or what you'd find interesting, or how you'd tease me about something."

He laced his fingers through Ashley's, giving her hand a squeeze. "I meant it, though," he added, more seriously. "I don't want to be like my dad was, and I'm not sure I know how not to be." Hockey was always going to be important, was going to dictate where Connor lived and how much time he had to devote to someone else.

"I know how important hockey is for you and I don't want it *not* to be. I don't think hockey and a relationship are in the same category. You *can* have both." And somehow when Ashley said it, it sounded like it was *true*. It gave Connor hope in a way that was also *scary*.

Another squeeze of Ashley's hand drew his attention back to the conversation. "These past two months, I haven't felt like I came second to hockey and we weren't even dating for real. Did you feel like having me in your life interfered with your work?"

Because it was Ashley asking, Connor actually took the

time to think about it, and didn't just jump to the answer he thought she wanted to hear. "No," he admitted, shaking his head. "You've made some parts of work easier, with the way you've handled all the press stuff." Connor *knew* his image was better now than it had been, and it hadn't even been *bad* before.

"And you don't interfere with playing or training," he continued because Ashley never had. "But wouldn't it be different if we were really dating? Wouldn't you *mind*?" Connor did believe Ashley when she said she didn't want hockey not to be important, but his mom would've said the same about his dad, that she hadn't wanted his career not to be important. Connor knew it had still made her sad when he'd canceled their plans together, or not turned up to something she'd mentioned ten times.

"I'm not sure why it would be different. I'd still want you to do what made you happy." It sounded so *simple* when she said it. "I can't promise that things will always work out but... I'd like to give it a go, Connor. And it seems like maybe so would you? We could always just be scared together?" The offer was followed by a small smile.

"You make being scared sound pretty good," Connor teased, lifting a hand to brush his thumb against the corner of Ashley's smile. "Yeah, I'd like to give it a go, too." Ashley was right, they couldn't guarantee anything, but they could *try* being together. If their fake relationship was anything to go by, they should do pretty well.

There were probably a dozen questions Connor should have asked. What about Dallas? Were they going to keep pretending they'd been together for months? Were they going to keep pretending to be soulmates?

Instead of asking any of those things, Connor bent his head to brush his lips against Ashley's, free hand settling on her waist as she opened her mouth under his.

CHAPTER EIGHT

Ashley

Connor's lips felt just as good against Ashley's as she remembered them from the night of the gala. Hot and hard in exactly the right sort of ways. The worry she felt seemed to ease, especially as Connor cupped Ashley's face, the kiss deepening with his tongue against her lips. Parting them, she let him in, licking back just as a soft moan escaped her. God, had she wanted this then and she wanted it *now*.

Ashley's hand came up to brush over Connor's neck and she kissed him back harder, enjoying the eager response he gave. When she came up for air, Ashley's breath caught slightly at just how hot Connor looked.

"I'm sorry I'm in my pjs, I wasn't expecting... Maybe I should go change," Ashley said with a frown, glancing over at her bedroom door. At least at the gala, she had felt *sexy*. The dress she'd been in had been beautiful and Connor had *said* she'd looked hot. Now Ashley was wearing loose pjs and her hair was a mess.

"No," Connor said. The hand on Ashley's waist tugged her closer like he couldn't bear the thought of her moving away from him for even a minute. "You look great." He did pull back.

Ashley could feel his gaze roving over her, making her cheeks flush. Connor didn't *look* disappointed. The hand in her hair moved gently, pushing it behind her ear.

"Relaxed, but beautiful," he assured. Ashley felt it might be best to believe him, especially as the next thing he did was kiss her again, teeth catching against her lower lip while his hand moved teasingly over her waist. His touch was firm, not ticklish at all, not even when his fingers slipped under Ashley's loose t-shirt to seek out the skin.

Not having as *complicated* clothing between them as they had at the gala meant that it was much easier for Connor's hands to brush over Ashley's stomach. It was also much easier for her hands to slide under Connor's shirt, her tongue still working its way into his mouth. When Connor's fingers hit a particularly sensitive spot, Ashley moaned, pressing in closer.

Pulling back for a breath, Ashley gave Connor a grin. She knew she wanted this, wanted him. Even at the gala, she hadn't fully allowed herself to think she could *have* this. Now, though, that was the thought that kept running through her head. That and how much she wanted to see Connor shirtless, to touch each and every muscle with her tongue.

Crawling into Connor's lap, Ashley grazed her teeth over his jaw. Her hands slid between them to seek out the hem of Connor's shirt so she could pull it up.

Very obligingly, Connor pulled back, holding his arms up and letting Ashley lift the shirt over his head. She barely even noticed where she dropped it, too captivated by the hard muscles that shifted under Connor's skin. He looked so *strong*, with only a light dusting of chest hair that thickened into a trail leading down into his jeans.

Before Ashley could decide just where she wanted to put her mouth first, Connor's hands were back on her, impatiently tugging her own shirt over her head. "Fuck," Connor growled. The sheer amount of desire in his voice went straight between Ashley's legs.

Connor leaned in, biting gently at her shoulder while his

fingers teased along the curves of Ashley's breasts.

A shiver run over Ashley's back but then Connor's hand followed it, leaving a warm tingle in its wake instead. Moving forward, Ashley pressed her breasts against Connor's chest as she leaned to capture his lips with her again. His kisses were as hot as his hands. Ashley rocked against Connor, pleased to find him getting hard against her.

"Carry me to the bedroom?" Ashley asked, certain that Connor *could* and wanting to experience it. He was strong, and there was something *very* appealing about having Connor use that strength to move Ashley. When he did lift her, straight up from the position they were in, Ashley gave a very loud squee, before giggling. "This is very sexy," she informed Connor, but it didn't make her sound any less amused.

Connor laughed, and that only seemed to make Ashley feel hotter as she wrapped her arms around his neck. "It's very sexy from where I'm standing, too," Connor promised, taking the opportunity to give Ashley's backside a squeeze. Though he'd never been to her bedroom before, Ashley's apartment was small enough for Connor to find it easily, and he dropped her down softly against the sheets.

He didn't waste time, following Ashley and pressing his body against hers. One hand lifted to her breast, cupping it gently. When his fingers found her nipple, he rolled it, making Ashley whimper against his mouth as Connor kissed her again. Through his jeans, Connor's erection felt long and thick. Before Ashley could think about getting her hands on him, Connor was kissing his way down her body.

"Wanted to do this since the moment I saw you in that dress," he said. His stubble scratched between Ashley's breasts before he drew one nipple into his mouth.

Another moan fell from Ashley's lips, her hand finding Connor's hair. Fingers tangling in it, Ashley gave a small tug, only to follow it by pulling Connor's head closer against her. She gave a sharp cry of pleasure when Connor moved to suck her other nipple into his mouth. Knowing that he'd wanted this, that he'd thought about it, it made Ashley feel even hotter.

With her free hand, Ashley reached to drag her nails gently over Connor's back and shoulders. His tongue swirling around her nipple made her moan. Connor bit it lightly making Ashley's nails dig sharply into his skin.

Connor's groan of pleasure vibrated against Ashley's breast, sending tingles all the way to her core. Giving the other nipple a parting bite, Connor moved to kiss lower. He paused, circling his tongue teasingly around her navel while his fingers brushed at the waistband of Ashley's pajama pants.

"Can I?" he asked, looking up at her. His expression was so sincere that Ashley had no doubt he *would* have stopped if she had asked him to. It was sweet, and not at all undermined by the way Connor rocked his erection against Ashley's leg.

"Yeah," she breathed, unable to even imagine what might make her say that Connor should stop. Just the idea of having Connor's mouth against her made Ashley's body feel on fire. When he hooked his fingers against Ashley's waistband, she lifted her hips to help Connor get her pj bottoms off.

Ashley's fingers tugged against Connor's hair, the anticipation of having his mouth against her building. There was another soft moan that escaped Ashley when Connor ran his tongue over her inner thigh. "Fuck, you look so good between my legs," she sighed, very honestly and very turned on.

Connor grinned up at her, amusement and desire both twinkling in his eyes. Whatever he might have said in response, he clearly decided that there were better uses he could put his mouth to. Ashley felt his tongue, wet and hot, lapping against her sensitive flesh. His strong fingers spanned Ashley's hips, pinning her against the sheets.

Ashley moaned as Connor's tongue licked harder against her, gathering up the wetness that had built in her anticipation. If possible, he looked even better, his expression so concentrated. Ashley could *feel* the way he responded to what she liked. Anything that made her cry out, Connor repeated again, and again, making sure he knew how to get a reaction out of her before he moved to try something new.

Sucking her lower lip between her teeth, Ashley moaned in response to the magic that Connor was doing with his tongue. With one hand in Connor's hair, Ashley moved her other hand above her to grip the bed frame, knuckles whitening. "Fuck, yes, that's nice," she moaned rocking her hips against Connor's face. With his hand holding her hips down she didn't have much room to do so. He nonetheless rewarded her by running his tongue over her clit.

"Connor!" Ashley cried out. Her fingers tightened in his hair, tugging as if to draw him in even closer.

Connor slowed down, the touch of his tongue steady and firm. Releasing one of Ashley's hips, he brought a hand between her legs. One finger circled teasingly at Ashley's entrance in a way that almost made her clamp her thighs around his wrist. The ache to have something inside her - to have *Connor* inside her - felt overwhelming.

In response to her noises, Connor managed to smirk up at her, without ever moving his tongue from her clit. Despite his apparent patience, Ashley could hear his breath coming harsh and hard. It only made her feel more confident in how much he wanted her.

A rather loud 'fuck' fell from Ashley's lips when one of Connor's fingers pressed inside her. She already felt so hot and wet, easily pushing down against him. He took it for the encouragement that it was, licking against her faster until Ashley could feel her stomach muscles tightening. Connor's mouth was going to make her come and she was pretty sure that was precisely what he was aiming for.

Gripping harder against the headboard, Ashley rocked her hips more, the sounds falling from her lips increasing in volume. A string of 'yes', 'yes', 'yesssss' followed and finally, Ashley's orgasm crashed over her, leaving all of the nerve-endings in her body tingling. She trailed her hand down lower from Connor's hair to his neck, before letting her nails scratch over his shoulder lightly in an attempt to pull him back up so she could kiss him.

His hands skimmed over her body as he rose to meet her. Kissing her slowly, he let Ashley enjoy the weight of him pressing her down into the mattress. She could feel how hard he was, his hips rocking gently against her thigh. She pressed back harder, making Connor groan.

He sucked against her lower lip, teeth pressing into it none-too-gently. He was struggling to hold himself back. He kept one hand between her legs, fingers still teasing at her entrance.

"Ashley," he breathed, "I want you so much." He traced his tongue over his lips, eyes going dark as he tasted Ashley still on them. "Have you got a condom? I didn't think *this* was going to happen." He gave her a grin that made Ashley laugh out loud.

The laugh seemed to ease whatever tension she had been feeling - and really, Ashley hadn't even realized she *had* - and she gave a nod. "Yeah, yeah, I have a condom," she said. Somewhat unwillingly she pushed Connor off her so she could reach for the bedside table. It didn't take her long to find a condom and when she turned back, Ashley's breath audibly caught at the sight of Connor.

He'd wiggled himself out of the rest of his clothes, now lying there naked. With his broad shoulders and athletic built, Connor looked *stunning.* Ashley was struck again by just how much she wanted to lick all over his body. Deciding that there was no reason *not to*, Ashley pressed a kiss - and then a small bite - against Connor's shoulder, before licking her way down his chest.

The noises Connor made, especially as Ashley paused to pay attention to one of his nipples, made no secret of his enjoyment. He moaned, his hips bucking off the bed as he sought some kind of friction. "Ashley," he panted, and Ashley enjoyed how her name sounded in that desperate tone. "*Please.*"

One of his big hands rested on her shoulder, the other clenched in the sheets. Ashley continued to tease him, licking every line of muscle, loving the way Connor writhed beneath her. Now there were no clothes left between them, Ashley could feel the heat that poured off Connor's skin. His erection pressed hard against her stomach as she wriggled her way down his body, making him choke on a moan.

She'd wanted to trace his muscles with her mouth for what felt like *ages*, so Ashley took her time to at least make a beginning. Her lips were soft but hot against Connor's stomach. The way he tried to buck up but couldn't because her body trapped him beneath her was incredibly hot. Ashley moved lower to let her breasts brush over his cock, smirking up at Connor a little when he groaned loudly.

Connor's cock slid between her breasts and Ashley paused briefly so he could enjoy that before she ran her hands over Connor's hips. Pressing a kiss against the base of Connor's stomach, Ashley glanced up at him. His expression looked so good. Ashley licked her lips, wanting nothing more than to make it even *more* blissed out.

With her tongue darting out, Ashley leaned in to lick over the tip of Connor's cock, parting her lips when he bucked up to meet her touch.

His grunt of surprise quickly turned into a satisfying moan of pleasure as Ashley hollowed her cheeks around his length. Connor's cock was *big*. Ashley had to wrap the fingers of one hand around the base of it to keep him from overwhelming her as he thrust up into her mouth. Connor's rhythm was steady, but not fast. Judging by the white-knuckled hand fisted in the sheets, he was in no rush for this to be over.

With her free hand, Ashley explored Connor's abs. Every time the muscles contracted under her touch, she felt a similar tightening in her core, and Connor's groans grew louder. "Fuck, you feel so good," Connor breathed. His fingers stroked through Ashley's hair, coming to rest on the back of her head. He didn't push her down, but Ashley could feel him there, and it made her *want* to take him deeper.

Tilting her head slightly, Ashley took in as much of Connor as she could, enjoying the small sound of surprise he gave before it was followed by a much louder one of pleasure. Moving up and down a few times, Ashley pulled back. Licking her lips, she undid the condom wrapper before sliding the condom on. She gave Connor's cock one more teasing lick, before shifting back so she could crawl up Connor's body.

When his hands came to settle against Ashley's hips, she grinned down at him. With legs on each side of Connor, Ashley reached between them to lead his cock into her. She was slow at lowering herself onto him, soft moans falling from her lips as she adjusted to his size. Once he was fully in her, Ashley leaned forward to kiss Connor, before rocking her hips and letting both of their moans mix together.

Connor let Ashley set the pace, his thrusts matching Ashley's movements almost perfectly. When she pulled back, she could feel Connor's gaze on her. There was obvious desire in his eyes as he watched her breasts bounce while she rode him slowly. Lifting one hand to her breast, Connor rubbed his thumb across her nipple, giving Ashley a smug smirk when her breath caught in her throat.

Without hesitation, Connor leaned forward, catching Ashley's nipple between his lips. His tongue circled around it in a way that made pleasure shoot straight between Ashley's legs. One hand moved to tug against her other nipple, and the other moved to cup Ashley's ass, urging her on as she rolled her hips to take him deeper.

A soft gasp escaped Ashley as she began to increase the pace. Knowing that Connor had plenty of strength, that he could've easily taken over but *didn't*, it somehow made Ashley feel so much hotter. She had more power over what they were doing and it felt *good*. With her hips moving faster, Ashley rode Connor harder, enjoying when the sound he made in response vibrated through her body.

"Fuck, Connor," Ashley cried. Her fingers tangled in Connor's hair as she pulled him closer against her breast. It felt amazing, the way his tongue circled her nipple *and* the way his cock filled her up. The hand on her ass pushed Ashley up and then came back with her, as if to offer *support* rather than dictate anything.

When Ashley's muscles tightened around him, Connor groaned, his hand squeezing her ass in encouragement. He bit lightly at her nipple, before soothing the jolt of pain with his tongue, lapping hot and wet at the sensitive tip. Ashley moved faster, making no attempt to hold back the moans that filled the room.

Connor's hips pushed up harder, still matching her pace, but with more force. It drove his cock deeper inside her, and they both groaned. Connor's sounds vibrating against Ashley's breast. He pulled back, still tugging her other nipple between his fingers. "You're so gorgeous," he said, with a smile that turned quickly into a smirk. "I think I want to watch you come again." He traced his fingers over Ashley's hip until he could tease them over her inner thigh.

Ashley was most definitely not going to *discourage* Connor from making her come again. She used her hands to pull him in closer against her, rocking her hips forward to meet the finger he pressed between her legs. The pleasures mixed together and Ashley could easily feel her orgasm building. She moved harder and faster. Before long, Connor's name fell from her lips in half a scream as pleasure shot through her.

Crushing her lips against Connor's, Ashley kissed him *hard* before pulling back breathlessly. "Fuck, you feel so good," she told him, her body still sensitive from the orgasm she'd just experienced. Ashley didn't slow down in riding Connor, wanting to experience his climax. Wanting to *see* it on his face.

His hips bucked up even harder to meet hers, both hands on her back, holding her crushed close against his muscular chest. The noises Connor made grew louder and louder. With a groan, he *flipped* them, pinning Ashley to the mattress under them. Connor didn't miss a beat, thrusting hard and fast. Ashley watched his eyes roll back as pleasure overwhelmed him.

Pulling her close, Connor muffled his moan in her shoulder, teeth nipping at her skin. She felt him give one last, deep thrust as he came. His hips slowed, and eventually stopped, still snug against hers. He ran a hand over her side, waking aftershocks of pleasure along every nerve-ending. Connor hummed, nuzzling at her shoulder, and clearly making an effort not to crush Ashley under beneath his weight. "I don't want to move now," he said, voice low and rough. "Can I stay?"

Ashley gave a small laugh at the question. *Of course* she wanted him to stay. She also felt fairly confident that that's what Connor wanted. "Yes," she nodded, pressing a kiss against his lips. When Connor did finally move, it was to quickly dispose of the condom before he cuddled against Ashley's side. She hadn't anticipated that he'd want cuddling, but it definitely wasn't unwelcome.

Dragging her finger slowly over Connor's arm, Ashley smiled. This was *nice*. It felt good, right almost. She traced upwards until her finger caught against a loose corner of Connor's soulmark sticker. The realization that Connor really might be her soulmate struck Ashley suddenly. She was more surprised by how *not terrible* it felt.

"We're awful at fake dating," she announced.

Connor lifted his head to look at her, his expression soft and relaxed in a way Ashley hadn't seen before. He smiled, before giving her an exaggerated frown. "I think that's a very negative way to look at it," he teased. "You could just as easily say we're so *good* at fake dating that we ended up doing it for real."

Ashley paused, giving Connor's suggestion actual thought. She knew he was teasing but Ashley did wonder if maybe Connor was right. They had done *very* well at fake dating, miles better than Ashley had done in any of her actual relationships. Tugging lightly against the sticker, Ashley waited for Connor to stop her. When he didn't, she pulled it off, revealing the soulmark.

With a finger softly tracing over the letters, Ashley gave Connor a smile. "I think you're right," she said finally. "Do you think the same is true about us being fake soulmates?"

There was definitely a pause. It was only the way Connor

leaned into her touch that kept Ashley from starting to feel nervous. When he did speak, it was slowly, as if thinking through every word.

"I don't know." Connor propped himself up a little against Ashley's pillows, reaching out to brush his hand over *her* mark. "There are a lot of Connors, and a lot of Ashleys," he pointed out. "I don't know how you *know* if you've found the right one."

He frowned slightly, only stopping when Ashley lifted a hand to touch the crease between his brows. "My parents had matching soulmarks," Connor told her, and Ashley realized it wasn't something he'd said before. "They weren't happy. I don't know if that means they *aren't* soulmates, or if it means soulmates don't always work out."

Ashley was hardly going to be the person who argued that they *must* be soulmates, especially because she did agree with Connor that there was a chance they *weren't*. But Ashley was willing to entertain the idea which was a great deal more than she would've expected herself to.

"I think that for a lot of people it's very hard to admit when things aren't working, especially once you've convinced yourself this is it, you've met your soulmate," Ashley commented. She rolled over on her stomach so she could look at Connor more easily. This seemed like a conversation that required looking at each other.

"And yeah, maybe we won't work out, but I'm willing to give it a shot if you are." The idea that he might *not* almost physically ached inside of Ashley. She also wanted to believe that he did want this. Connor had given her no indications that he didn't.

"Of course I am," Connor agreed. He looked almost shocked by the idea that he might *now* decide he wasn't willing to give it a go. "Whether you might be my soulmate or not, I'd want to give this a go," he clarified. He reached out, running a hand through Ashley's hair softly, teeth pressing down into his lower lip.

"It is a bit scary that you might be," he admitted. "Just

because -" He paused, and Ashley let him get his thoughts into order without interrupting. "I don't know, I guess it seems like a lot of pressure." Ashley could certainly see that, especially given how *public* their matching soulmarks were. "Everyone thinks we've known each other for months longer than we have," Connor elaborated. "And what about Dallas?"

Ashley *was* still going to Dallas in a couple of months' time, so that was a very fair question to ask. Like how hockey mattered to Connor, Ashley's career mattered to her. She didn't, however, think it *couldn't* work. If they worked for it, they could have the best of both worlds.

"You're an NHL superstar," Ashley teased. "I'm sure you can afford to fly your girlfriend out for a weekend or so." She didn't think Connor would be against it. In the time she'd known him, Connor hadn't been *shy* about spending money.

She did give him a much softer smile, too, though. "I think taking a risk that it might not work, this thing between us, that's part of what makes it worth doing."

Connor chuckled. "Somehow, it doesn't surprise me that the risk appeals to you," he noted. "Obviously I was right when I said you're unlikely to choose the easy route." He moved down on the bed to join Ashley, turned onto his side so he could still see her. His hand stroked down her bare side. It raised goosebumps on Ashley's skin, and not from the cold.

"A weekend or so doesn't seem very much," he said, looking more serious. "I already miss you when I have to be away for games."

"And I miss you," Ashley said easily. "But I like it when I do see you." It seemed pretty simple. Sure, Ashley would rather she didn't have to leave, but she was hardly the sort of person who wanted to sacrifice one thing she loved for another. It wasn't *ideal* but it was a challenge. As Connor had pointed out, Ashley *liked* risk and she definitely liked challenges.

Shuffling in closer to Connor, Ashley pressed a kiss against his lips. "Maybe if you play your cards right, I'll send you some nudes," Ashley teased.

The sound Connor made - halfway between a laugh and a moan - was honestly delightful. Ashley beamed at him. "Well, when you put it like that," he teased. The hand that had been innocently running along Ashley's side moved down to her ass, cupping it as Connor pulled her closer to kiss her back.

It was a much slower kiss than the ones they'd shared earlier. Connor seemed determined to explore Ashley's mouth. He sucked on her lower lip as he pulled back, his breath coming faster. "Do we keep up the story that we met five months ago?" he asked. "It seems... easier. And it's not as if anyone but us is really going to *care* exactly when we met."

"It does seem easier," Ashley nodded. There was no reason for them *not* to, really. "You'll have to tell everyone who knows the truth," she pointed out, but Ashley hardly imagined that to be an issue. If anything, it seemed kind of... *nice* that they'd developed real feelings for each other.

Ashley ran her hand down over Connor's broad back. Even there she could feel muscles move and Ashley had to admire just how *beautiful* Connor truly was. She'd known he was great looking, but that had been *clothed*. He was unbelievably hot naked.

"You're so fucking hot," she breathed, because, really, Connor just *was*.

"Look who's talking," Connor said, grinning at Ashley like he truly believed she was every bit as hot as he was. He smoothed a hand down over Ashley's ass, fingers curving around her thigh before he hitched her leg up. It brought their hips flush together, and Connor ground against her eagerly.

"I *thought* I was sleepy," he announced, "but all this talking has woken me up again." His mouth dropped to Ashley's neck, and he bit down on the skin over her collarbone, making Ashley's breath catch in a gasp. "What shall I do with all this energy?" Connor asked, barely lifting his mouth from her skin long enough for her to make out the words.

"Oh, I don't know," Ashley said rocking into Connor's touch. "Have you considered reading?" She teased, but her actions were very far from suggesting that she planned for Connor to stop to *read* right now. Rather, as her hands trailed down Connor's back, Ashley felt her actions were suggesting he do something a lot more active than that.

CHAPTER NINE

Connor

C onnor had supposed that dating Ashley for real would feel basically the same as dating her for the press. He hadn't expected just how differently it would affect him emotionally. Ashley still came to the Howlers' games, but now it filled Connor's chest with pride to know she was out there, seeing him do what he did best. She still teased him, and she still explained things in a way that Connor understood, but both came with an undercurrent of affection that lifted Connor's spirits far beyond what he'd been used to when Ashley was only *pretending*.

He'd told Maisy first. She'd laughed so hard she'd had to hang up, and only congratulated him when she rang back later in the evening. She hadn't *said* so, but Connor knew she was withholding judgment on the whole soulmate part of his and Ashley's relationship. That was fine. Connor was kind of waiting for more evidence either way, too. He didn't care if Ashley *wasn't* his soulmate, because he still had fun with her. The more he realized how deeply his moods were connected to Ashley's presence in his life, the more Connor hoped that maybe Ashley *was*, that this would be the relationship that didn't fizzle out.

His mum, as Connor had expected, was over the moon.

"Oh, Connor!" she sighed at him over their regular Tuesday call. "It's so romantic! Like something you'd read in a magazine."

"Like something *you'd* read in a magazine," Connor corrected playfully. It made him think. Ashley had said that people wanted to believe celebrities were living the perfect, more enchanted life. Meeting his soulmate while looking for a *pretend* soulmate did feel like it was somehow... more. Connor made a mental note to talk it through with Ashley, later.

"When do I get to meet her?" Liz asked, and Connor grinned. He *wanted* that, for Ashley to meet his mom, and Maisy. He wanted them all to discover what he loved about each of them.

"I don't know, mom," he hedged. As much as Connor looked forward to it, he and Ashley had only *really* been dating for a week, and that seemed pretty soon for the meeting of the family. "If the Howlers make it to the playoffs, you'll come to watch some of the games, right? And I'm sure Ashley will." He could hear his mom's laugh down the phone and knew what she'd say almost before she said it.

"Must *everything* in your life revolve around hockey?" she asked. Connor didn't need to see her to know she was rolling her eyes.

"Yup," Connor agreed, without guilt. They moved on, his mom telling him all the latest gossip from home.

Three weeks after Connor and Ashley decided to make things real, the Howlers lost a game. They should have easily won, and what was worse was that there was no real *reason*. No one was injured, there'd been only a normal amount of on-ice aggression, and there was no obvious hole in their defensive line. Every small thing that *could* go badly had done, from a pass being intercepted to Connor *missing* when he'd had a clean shot at the goal.

The mood in the locker room after was low. The team did what they always did, hurrying through interviews and press attention so they could all go home to sulk in peace.

Connor had been in his living room for nearly an hour, mentally replaying every wrong move and missed goal, when it occurred to him that for the first time, he didn't *need* to be alone. He hadn't messaged Ashley, because he hadn't really wanted to *talk*, but of course, Ashley had been at the game herself, she'd already *seen* how badly it had gone.

He sent her a text immediately, offering to pay for an Uber over.

By the time she arrived, Connor still felt pretty grim. He did manage to find a smile for her. "Sorry it took so long," he apologized. "I guess I'm not used to having someone who won't mind being around me after we lose."

Ashley tiptoed to kiss Connor and somehow that already made the tightness in his chest ease. Not so much he'd forget about the loss tonight, but at least to relieve it a bit. "I don't mind," she confirmed, taking Connor's hand so she could squeeze it. "We can cuddle on the sofa and make you feel better, yeah? Have you eaten?"

The question honestly took Connor by surprise. He *never* ate after a loss. At least, not since he'd moved to Madison, and started living by himself. "No," he said, shaking his head. "Not since before the game. I don't really feel hungry." Despite that, Connor did lead the way to the kitchen, offering Ashley her choice from the drinks in his fridge.

"I'll feel better tomorrow," he promised, which was *probably* true. Tomorrow there would be training, and Connor always felt better after he could get out on the ice. It was hard to let failure go before he had an opportunity to prove he could do better. "Not that I'm saying no to cuddles," he added. It *did* make his heart feel lighter to think about having Ashley in his arms for a while.

"Take a seat, I'll make you something light," Ashley instructed. "Egg white omelet. The protein will do you good." The way she said it didn't leave much room for argument and that kind of felt... nice. Connor didn't have to think too hard, Ashley would take care of it. Of him. He watched her move around the kitchen, getting the eggs, setting the frying pan up, just letting Connor be there with her.

Once the food was ready, Ashley set the plate down in front of Connor and then pressed a kiss against his cheek. "You can feel better tomorrow, but today you can feel bad."

The words freed Connor from any expectation that he had to be good company. He was surprised to find that made it easier to look on the bright side. He chuckled, reaching out a hand to catch hold of Ashley's shirt, keeping her close. "I like having you here," he told her. It was true, but it also made Connor's heart ache, because Ashley wasn't always going to *be* there. She was going to be in Dallas, hours and hours away. It made Connor feel almost *worse* than losing had.

So he wouldn't say anything about how he wished Ashley didn't have to go, Connor took a forkful of the omelet. It was pretty good. The first bite made Connor realize how *hungry* he'd been. "How is it that you know just what to do and just what to say?" he asked. "Do you think it's a soulmate thing?"

Ashley stilled and briefly, Connor had to wonder if that hadn't been the right thing to say. When she gave him a smile, it felt *reassuring*. "Maybe it is," she nodded. Obviously, Ashley, like Connor, couldn't say for certain, but the fact that she would at least entertain the idea made Connor feel *good*. He knew Ashley's opinions on soulmates, so to know that she was willing to consider him hers was *important*.

"Or maybe I'm just a very good girlfriend," Ashley teased.

"You are a very good girlfriend," Connor agreed, feeling a warmth settle in his stomach that had nothing to do with being fed. "I guess I was wondering whether you're good at being a girlfriend *in general*, or if it's different with me." Connor *wanted* to believe that things were different with him, that Ashley hadn't always been this good at being part of a couple. As long as what they had was special, Connor didn't really *mind* whether they were soulmates or not. At least, he didn't *think* he did.

Taking another bite, Connor chewed thoughtfully before he offered, "It feels different for me. You don't try to make me guess what you want, or make me feel stupid when I can't." Those were qualities that Connor's previous girlfriends had lacked. "And it's easier to be open with you," he carried on. "I guess probably *because* I know you're open with me."

He saw her hesitate and it really just went to illustrate Connor's point. In the past, if a girlfriend had reacted like that, Connor would've rushed in to say she didn't have to answer or apologize for *whatever* might've upset her. But with Ashley, Connor knew she'd *tell him*. It might take her a moment to find the right words and that was... pretty great, really. To know that she'd be honest, that she'd explain.

"I don't think most of my exes would say I'm a good girl-friend," Ashley finally said, turning away to tidy the dishes she'd used to make Connor a meal. "You've been... you haven't seemed like you mind it when I take charge. Other men I've dated be-fore, they didn't really *like* that I wanted to plan things, or that I always needed to have a structure to what was going on."

The way she looked, as if she were ashamed of having to admit that other men might not have liked her, was almost physically painful. Connor got up, reaching out to tug her close to him, one arm around her waist.

"I think it's great when you take charge," he told her, try-ing to keep a lid on his emotions so that he didn't sound as fierce as he felt. "You've made things run much more smoothly than I could ever hope to. Why wouldn't I like that?"

Part of Connor wanted to find out who these men were who'd made Ashley feel bad for being herself, so he could tell them how wrong they were. *More* of him was just glad to be the one Ashley was with now.

Lifting one hand to Ashley's cheek, Connor tipped her face up to his, brushing his lips across hers. He'd meant it to be just a light kiss, brief because he certainly wasn't used to wanting anything *more* in the kind of mood he was in. Ashley's lips were so soft, her body warm against his, that Connor found himself deepening the kiss out of pure instinct.

Ashley kissed back, her lips parting to let Connor slide his tongue in, meeting it with her own. Her hand came to brush over Connor's side before Ashley pulled back, giving him what looked like a rather suspicious look. "Are you trying to distract me or yourself?" She asked. Her tone was teasing enough that Connor knew he wasn't really expected to answer it. If he'd had to, the answer was probably 'both'.

"You need to finish your food," Ashley informed him. "And then we can go cuddle on the couch." The authority in her voice made Connor grin, but he didn't talk back. Instead, he returned to finish off his food and then let Ashley lead them through to the living room. She kicked her shoes off and pressed up against Connor's side once they'd sat down, shifting her legs to drape them over Connor's lap. It was strikingly *companionable*.

Reaching for the remote, Ashley clicked the TV on. "What are you in the mood for?" She asked before frowning slightly. "What sort of TV do you even like?"

Connor shrugged. The truth was that he was mostly in the mood for whatever he could watch mindlessly. He'd spend more of his time watching Ashley than the television. "I don't really watch much TV," he admitted. "I like films or something where I can sit down and watch from start to end. Somehow, I never seem to finish a TV series. Even with Netflix, I get distracted after an episode and I wander off. Then the next time I actually have a long enough break to watch TV in, I've forgotten what happened." Connor didn't really *mind.* Hockey had always been more important than staying up to date with the latest episode of whatever.

"You can pick," Connor offered, feeling that Ashley would probably *like* being given the control, even over something as trivial as what to watch on TV. "As long as it's not sports." Connor did watch sports, but not after he'd just lost a game. While Ashley clicked through a few different channels, Connor settled his weight comfortably against the couch. "I like documentaries," he admitted, shyly. It wasn't the kind of thing he'd tell the guys, so only his family really knew - and even they found it *surprising.*

Ashley, too, seemed surprised if the way she turned to look at him was any sort of indication. But then her face lit up in a wide smile that made Connor feel *good* about his admission. "What sort of documentaries?" She asked sounding genuinely interested in finding out. "Do you like animal documentaries? Those aren't too hard to watch even when you're tired."

Connor nodded his agreement, while also trying to decide how to answer the broader question. "Animal documentaries are good," he confirmed, "or anything about a person. I started out watching documentaries about sports, or about athletes." *That* part, at least, was unlikely to surprise anyone. "Then I started watching things about historical figures. Elvis, JFK."

Pausing, Connor considered whether to elaborate. It would have been easy to stop there, let Ashley believe there was an academic side to Connor that he'd been hiding all this time. It wouldn't have been *true*, and Connor wanted Ashley to know the truth, no matter how much that might change her opinion. "Sometimes I do fall asleep to the more boring ones," he admitted first. There was a certain tone of droning voice that lulled Connor to sleep like nothing else. "And I'm not very good at remembering all the facts from them." Connor didn't think watching documentaries made him any more *clever* than if he hadn't.

Whatever Connor might've anticipated Ashley's reaction to be, it wasn't the way she lightly bumped his arm with her hand to make him look at her and then give him a smile. "I fall asleep watching documentaries, too," she assured. "And no one can remember all the facts." She sounded so sure of herself, like there was no room for disagreement and somehow that made this feel better.

Clicking through to Netflix, Ashley selected one of the animal documentaries and once it was on, she cuddled closer to Connor. "This is nice. Maybe we can make this a tradition for the very rare occasions you lose?"

Connor smiled, both at Ashley's confidence that losing was a rare event and at the thought of having a tradition with her. "Yeah," he agreed, wrapping one arm around Ashley's shoulders and dropping a kiss against her hair. "We'll have to do it at other times, too," he pointed out, his playful tone proving just how much better he felt for having Ashley there. "Otherwise I'll start losing games just so I get to cuddle with you." Connor wouldn't really, of course. He doubted Ashey would object to them watching animal documentaries on normal evenings.

The documentary was just getting going when Connor realized, with an almost physical shock, that of course, this *couldn't* be their tradition when he lost, because Ashley wasn't going to *be* here. It made Connor feel moody all over again. "I guess, when you're in Dallas, we can watch together over Skype." It didn't feel at all as good, but it would have to be better than nothing.

"Yeah," Ashley nodded and there was an easiness in her tone that Connor didn't really share. "Or FaceTime, or even just the phone," she listed, nudging Connor's arm again so he'd look at her. When he did, Ashley gave him a soft look. "I know it'll be harder, but we'll make it work." And again, there was a sort of confidence in her tone that Connor just couldn't share. He didn't know how she could be so sure.

Maybe it was just his mood. Connor doubted he'd feel any more positive tomorrow. It hurt to imagine sitting on the phone with Ashley, unable to touch her, to smell her perfume or see the way that she beamed up at him whenever she was pleased.

He opened his mouth to say something, then closed it again. If it *was* just his mood, there was no sense in bringing Ashley down with him. If his feelings did persist, he could always talk to her later. It would be harder, but it wasn't as though Connor felt it would be *impossible*. Unless Ashley wanted to stay in Dallas *forever*.

They hadn't talked about whether there was an end in sight. It was too early when they hadn't even been separated yet. Connor couldn't help but feel he might be more positive about the whole thing if he knew it was temporary.

"We will make it work," Connor said. That much, at least, they could agree on. Connor wasn't going to let something as trivial as distance get in the way of this now.

◆ ◆ ◆

Connor had felt an unusual level of dread at the thought of another series of away games. It was only *somewhat* lessened by the fact that the last of them was in Pittsburg, where Connor's mom still lived. She always made a point of taking him out for a pre-game walk. Supposedly it was to calm Connor's game day nerves, but mostly it gave them an excuse to catch up. Connor liked revisiting the places he'd walked as a kid.

"Don't try to lie to me," Liz chided, once Connor had repeated for the third time how he and Ashley had decided to date for real. "I know you miss her."

Connor really *did*. This was the longest he'd been away from Ashley since they'd met. Texting her just wasn't filling the hole in Connor's life.

"I called her yesterday, and we talked for almost an hour," Connor admitted, "but -" He sighed, and his mom made a gesture for him to carry on. "It's not the same," he said, and he *knew* he sounded whiny. Luckily, his mom was one of the people who'd put up with that in him. "I miss her *being* here."

Liz fixed him with a look before she said, "If what you mean it that you miss the sex -"

"*Mom!*" Connor was so scandalized that he laughed, feeling lighter than he had in days. "That *isn't* what I mean." Of course, he missed the sex, not that he was going to tell his mom as much, but it wasn't just that. "I don't know how to explain it," he grumbled.

"I get it," his mom offered, her tone far more sympathetic. "It's a new relationship, you want to be around each other all the time, isn't that right?" Slowly, Connor nodded, his brows furrowing.

"I want to be around her all the time," he said. He wasn't sure Ashley necessarily felt the same way. "I don't know if she misses me as much as I miss her." Ashley had *said* that she missed him. It wasn't that Connor didn't believe her, but it nagged at him. "She's so positive about how we'll be able to work everything out when she moves," he admitted. "Like it doesn't even bother her that we won't be together." It bothered Connor a lot. He had yet to actually confess as much *to* Ashley.

They turned a corner onto a quieter street, and Connor glanced over to find his mom watching him with a tiny smile. "Don't you think maybe Ashley's being positive *because* she worries about missing you?" Connor must have looked as confused as he felt because his mom laughed. "Sweetie, she's worrying about it, just as much as you are. She's trying to put a positive spin on it to make you both feel better."

It did sound like something Ashley would do. It eased an anxiety in Connor's stomach to think that Ashley wasn't looking forward to their separation as much as he'd thought.

"I wish she didn't have to go," he admitted. "There must be PR jobs she can do in Madison. Or somewhere nearer than *Dallas*. I don't even know how long she's going to be out there." Connor was sure he'd read somewhere that hopping between jobs didn't look good, that you ought to expect to stay in one place for at least a year or two. He couldn't imagine only seeing Ashley occasionally for a whole year.

"Have you talked about it?" Liz asked, and Connor shrugged.

"She thinks it'll be fine. I'll fly her out sometimes, and we'll talk on the phone." It felt so horribly inadequate to think that was all the contact that they'd have. "I can't ask her not to go." Connor had thought about it. He knew it wasn't right to ask Ashley to make such a drastic change to her plans, not when they hadn't really known each other all that long.

"Maybe you don't have to ask her," Liz suggested. "Maybe what you need to do is something to *show* her how much you miss her. I'm sure she'd appreciate knowing you care."

"You think she doesn't know I care?" Connor asked, confused. He'd assumed that Ashley knew. Even though they hadn't talked much about it, surely Ashley understood that Connor wasn't wild about the idea of her being away? "I guess you could be right," he mused. "I've been acting like it'll be fine because she has." Maybe Ashley had been acting like it would be fine because Connor had, too. She couldn't really *want* to move away from him, could she? Not if she liked him as much as Connor liked her.

"I know you're not sure yet, but if she *is* your soulmate, surely that means you're supposed to be together?" Liz asked. Connor tried to repress the smile that tugged at the corners of his mouth. Talking about soulmates with his mom was dangerous. Despite how badly her relationship with Connor's dad had turned out, Liz still believed that soulmarks could be relied upon. Connor had never quite agreed. The idea of Ashley being his soulmate made him both stupidly happy and unbearably nervous.

"Maybe," he hedged, "but Ashley doesn't believe in soulmates." It was more complicated than that. Ashley did think they *might* be each other's, but Connor knew she didn't necessarily believe that meant lasting happiness for them. Neither did Connor. At least, not *completely.* "She wouldn't change the plans she's made for work on the strength of my name being the same as her soulmark." *That* much, at least, Connor was certain of.

"But she could make new plans, couldn't she?" Liz asked. "She's attached to the plans she made, but if something happened to make her adapt, she could." It wasn't a point Connor had thought about. He could see how it might be true. Ashley *was* excited about Dallas, and she'd made a lot of plans for getting herself out there and getting settled. She was so good at making plans, though, that if she had to, Connor had no doubt she'd make new plans she was *just* as excited about.

If she *had* to.

❖ ❖ ❖

After the game, Connor thought a lot about what his mom had said. Showing Ashley, rather than telling her, how much he hated the idea of being away *sounded* appealing, but Connor didn't really know *how*.

He could buy her something, bring home some gift as a way of showing that he'd been thinking of her. Ashley *knew* he'd been thinking of her because Connor had sent her messages almost constantly. Besides, she didn't really seem the kind of girl who'd get all emotional over some flowers or a piece of jewelry. Connor liked that about her. She wasn't always angling for Connor to buy her things. She let him pay for meals and outings, but that made sense. Connor was a professional hockey player, while Ashley was a student working in a diner.

Big gestures had never really been Connor's strong point, despite his mom's obsession with love stories. He almost wished he could ask Ashley what he should do. He had no doubt that she would know. It would defeat the point of not *talking* about his feelings.

It stayed in Connor's mind that Ashley could make new plans. This job in Dallas wasn't the *only* thing that would make her happy. Actually, if she found *another* job, nearer Madison, wouldn't that make her happier? Connor didn't think he was being arrogant in assuming Ashley would've liked to stay close if she *could*.

Sat at their departure gate, ready to fly home, Connor scrolled through job ads for PR. He quickly realized that he had no idea what half the terms meant. There was no way he could judge what Ashley would consider a *good* job.

"Hey, Scott," Connor called. "What would you look for if you wanted a job managing the PR for a big brand?"

Crossing to take the seat next to Connor's, Scott gave him a puzzled look. "You thinking of quitting hockey, Lewis?" he teased, making Connor laugh.

"Fuck no. Hockey for life. It's for Ashley." That, if anything, made Scott look even *more* confused.

"I thought Ashley had a job lined up?" he asked. "I'm sure I've got an email in my inbox asking us for a reference."

"You have?" This was the first Connor had heard about it. He remembered Ashley saying she'd emailed the company in Dallas to let them know about her thesis.

"Yeah, they asked if we're impressed with her. I'm going to reply tomorrow, tell them that she's great." Scott grinned, and Connor felt his stomach churn. Ashley was great. She'd made Connor's image better than it had ever been, but Connor didn't *want* Scott to tell the people in Dallas about how great she was. It would mean Ashley *leaving*.

If only, just this once, someone could tell the employers in Dallas that Ashley *wasn't* great. Maybe they'd want to hire someone else. Then any future jobs - especially ones closer to Madison - would get to hear about Ashley being amazing.

A horrible idea struck Connor then. Why couldn't *he* tell Dallas that Ashley wasn't great? She'd worked with him the most, and as far as *they* knew, it was all a PR stunt. Connor could make it sound like she'd been difficult to work with, and they'd almost certainly believe him.

If the job in Dallas went away, Ashley would find a new job. She'd probably be *relieved* that she didn't have to move. She could stay in Madison - or at least, *closer* to Madison.

"Do you want me to talk to them?" Connor asked, almost before he'd really committed to a decision. "I've worked with her more closely than you have." It would be for the best - for *everyone*. Ashley and Connor could stay together, without having to rely on Skype and phone calls. They could explore whether they really were soulmates without having to wonder if being so far apart was messing everything up.

"Sure, if you want," Scott agreed readily. "I can forward you the email now, I'm sure they'd be glad to hear from you."

When the email came through, Connor read it carefully. He'd never had to write a reference for someone before, and he didn't really know where to start. Before he could worry too much about it, their flight was boarding. Connor's nerves were swept away by the excitement of getting to see Ashley again.

This was a good idea, he convinced himself. It would mean Ashley would *always* be there after Connor had been away. He spent the long hours of the flight drafting an email and sent it off as soon as he was home.

CHAPTER TEN

Ashley

The call had come early in the morning and Ashley had just gotten out of the shower. It hadn't been a long conversation. The point had been put across perfectly fine - Ashley's job offer had been withdrawn. When she'd asked why, the only explanation she'd been given was that they didn't think she'd be a good fit for the company. It didn't make *sense* and Ashley felt almost dizzy as she sat down on her bed.

For the past year, Ashley had worked so hard to be able to land this job. When it had come through she'd been *ecstatic*. It was such a great opportunity, it'd let her put a foot in the door for much bigger things in the future. Except now it wouldn't. Suddenly, Ashley was a month away from graduating and had no job to go into. She had already given notice at the diner, though maybe her boss would keep her on.

It wasn't what Ashley *wanted*, though. It certainly wasn't what she had *planned*. That was what finally pushed Ashley over the edge, the tears coming almost unstoppably. She'd just about managed to text Connor. It was nice to know that she could, that he'd come over and make her feel better. Because right now? Ashley really needed to feel better.

By the time Connor got there, Ashley had managed to stop crying, but her face was still puffy, eyes red as she let Connor in. Before he could even say anything Ashley had pulled Connor into a hug, already feeling better just for having his big arms hold her.

"I lost my job," she said when she finally pulled back. It was hard to even say it out loud without bursting into tears again.

Connor seemed almost as shocked as Ashley had been. He kept his arms wrapped around her, pressing a kiss against her hair. Ashley felt his warm hand on her back, rubbing soothing circles while he made wordlessly sympathetic noises.

When he did pull back, it was only far enough for him to cup Ashley's face, one hand tucking a strand of hair behind her ear. "I know it sucks," he said slowly, "but there will be other jobs, right?"

It was *logical*, of course, because yes, there would be other jobs. Ashley had wanted *this* job. She did take a step back to give Connor somewhat of a weak smile. "You're right," she nodded. Ashley didn't *feel* like Connor was right, but she knew he was. "I just don't..." Rather than finishing the sentence, Ashley sighed. She moved further into the apartment, Connor following her as she went.

Reaching for Connor's hand Ashley gave it a squeeze. "It's just that I had a plan, you know? And I thought they wanted me. This was going to be such a big step." The emotions edged closer once more, making Ashley sniffle again. She crawled on the sofa, pulling a pillow in close so she could hug it.

Connor followed her, clasping Ashley's hand between his big, warm palms. "I know," he agreed. "I know this isn't what you'd planned, and that's a lot to deal with." He squeezed Ashley's hand. "I know you, though. I know you'll come up with another plan that's just as good."

It was sweet, Connor's faith in her. Of course, he didn't really know anything about having a job outside of hockey. "There must be other companies," he carried on, sounding almost as though he was trying to convince *himself*. "Companies that can be a big step, too."

"It's really hard to get a good starter job," Ashley said with a small sigh. "I worked *really* hard to land this. They weren't even going to consider me before I did a postgraduate degree. Even then I had to sit three different tests to even get to the internship level." It was *frustrating* that they hadn't really given Ashley a *reason*. After all her hard work and after they had *offered her a job*.

Ashley couldn't help the way it just all suddenly felt so hopeless. "I just wish I knew what *happened*." It made Ashley feel pretty bad about the potential of getting a job when the one she had gotten had decided they didn't want her before she'd gotten a chance to actually work.

Connor was quiet. When Ashley turned to look at him, he had his lower lip caught between his teeth, almost as if he were nervous on her behalf. It didn't make a lot of sense. "I didn't realize it was so difficult," he said, and his expression was troubled.

"Don't you think it might be a good thing, in some ways?" Connor asked. "You might be able to get a job that's closer. There must be brands in Madison that need promotion." He gave Ashley a small smile. It sounded like he really was hopeful.

Ashley understood why Connor would assume that. Maybe she'd think so too if Ashley hadn't spent so long finding and then securing the right sort of a graduate position for herself. Still, she knew that Connor wanted her to be closer and that was sweet, so Ashley gave him a soft smile. "Yeah." Though she wasn't completely sure what it was referring to.

"I just wish I knew what went wrong. I thought they liked me for this and now I don't... I don't know what I did wrong, you know?" Except Connor probably didn't know. His career was very different from what Ashley had planned for hers.

"Maybe you didn't do anything wrong," Connor suggested. "Maybe they just... decided they didn't have the position that they thought they did." Except, Ashley knew that wasn't how this kind of job *worked*. "I don't think you should blame yourself when you didn't do anything wrong." He looked so seriously concerned, pulling Ashley closer and settling his hand against her waist.

"If you did well enough to get this job in the first place, isn't that a good sign that someone else will hire you?" He opened his mouth, as if to continue, and then stopped. "I don't know much about how PR works," he admitted. "I know it's important to you, as a career, and I get that. Is it important you get *this* job over any other?"

Ashley didn't really think she had the strength to continue this conversation. She got that Connor wanted to be supportive, but he just didn't *get it*. Yeah, he had worked hard to play for the NHL but it wasn't comparable to getting a job in the real world. To Connor it clearly seemed as easy as 'just get another job' and Ashley didn't think she could explain how it *wasn't* that easy.

"It was important to me," Ashley said, finally, her voice sounding as defeated as she felt. There was nothing she could do. The company that Ashley had wanted to work for didn't want her and that was that. It felt like such a massive blow, but apart from maybe figuring out why they no longer wanted her to work there, Ashley couldn't do anything else.

Wiping her face with the back of her hand, Ashley gave Connor a weak smile. "You want to watch some animal documentaries?"

Connor seemed to take a long time to reply, as if he were searching for the right words to say. Ashley would have helped, but in this situation, if there *were* right words, she had no more idea what they were than Connor seemed to.

"Yeah," he agreed, finally. "And I'll stay tonight, and make you breakfast in the morning. Hopefully, things won't feel so bad once you've slept on them." That made Ashley smile. She moved across the couch to cuddle into Connor. He was doing a great job of making her feel better, even if the upset wasn't going away completely.

Camellia Tate

◆ ◆ ◆

Things *didn't* look as bad the following day, but they didn't feel
great either. It helped a lot to have Connor's support, even if
Ashley could tell that he didn't quite know what to say. She
still appreciated that he'd come over, that he'd *tried*. Having left
Connor in bed with a note for when he woke up, Ashley headed
over to the Howlers' rink.

Scott had been nothing but helpful and nice to Ashley
since this thing with Connor had started, and as far as she could
tell he was very good at his job. Ashley was hopeful that he
might be able to advise her on what could've gone wrong with
the new job.

The rink wasn't very busy so early in the morning, mostly
because the team wasn't having a morning skate that day. Tex,
the security guy, recognized Ashley giving her a smile and a
'good morning' before opening the door for her. It was... nice.
Ashley could definitely see how the team - including everyone
who worked for them - acted like they were family.

Knowing her way to Scott's office, Ashley didn't need to
stop until she was there. She took a deep breath before knock-
ing. Thankfully, Scott was in, calling out for whoever knocked
to just come in. He looked up from whatever paperwork he was
working on, giving a surprised 'oh' when he saw Ashley.

"Sorry, I thought it was one of the guys. I'm waiting for
Ricky to show up and ask me to fix his Twitter mess," Scott
sighed in a way that Ashley assumed only a PR manager for an
NHL team could.

"No, just me. I won't keep you long," Ashley promised.
Scott shook his head, assuring her she could keep him as long as
she wanted, which made Ashley smile.

Taking a seat, she gave a soft sigh, which prompted Scott
to frown. "Is this about Connor? I thought you guys were doing
well?"

"We are," Ashley rushed to assure. "It's not about Connor." It really wasn't, which briefly made Ashley wonder if maybe she shouldn't have been here at all. She only knew Scott because of Connor. Maybe she shouldn't be coming to him for work-related advice. But then, Scott had always been very nice and he didn't seem like he minded when she told him it wasn't about Connor.

Ashley just felt a bit shaken up by everything that had happened. She recognized herself as being on edge about things right now. "It's about my job in Dallas," she explained.

"Oh yeah! Did Connor send them the reference?"

The question took Ashley by surprise and she frowned. Seeing her expression, Scott clarified, "I told him they'd asked, and he suggested that he should write one since the two of you had been working closely. I know it's a bit weird because you're also now dating, but I figured that'd just make him say nicer things, right?"

Ashley did get the logic but she also... Connor wouldn't have said *bad* things about her. There was no reason why he would've done that. It wasn't logical and Ashley was really struggling to figure out how to make sense of it.

"They withdrew the offer," Ashley said almost dumbly and Scott's eyes widened.

"What?" At least he sounded genuinely as shocked about it as Ashley had been when she'd received the call. It didn't take Scott long to start wondering about the same thing Ashley was. She could tell by how his expression changed. "You don't think that Connor..." But the way Scott stopped talking implied that he *too* thought that maybe Connor.

"I need to go," Ashley said getting up.

"Ashley," Scott stood, too. "I can try to give them a call." Ashley was sure that, like her, Scott knew these sorts of positions got filled almost before they emptied. It was a kind offer but not one that would bring any sort of a result.

"Thanks, Scott, but no, don't call them. It's... it's too late," Ashley shrugged. And yeah, it hurt, but she was almost too pre-occupied to think about how upset she was, her thoughts constantly returning to Connor. "Thanks again for all your help," she added almost in a daze before making her way back to her car.

◆ ◆ ◆

Ashley sat in her car for a while after she got back to the apartment block. Connor would probably be awake by now, making breakfast just as he'd promised. She could imagine it so easily. It would've warmed her heart if Ashley wasn't also so anxious about what she needed to ask Connor. The anxiety mixed in with anger, with such a deep sense of loss that Ashley almost didn't know what to do with it.

Except the obvious answer was to challenge Connor on it. Maybe it was just silly. Maybe there was another explanation. Ashley even entertained the idea that maybe he had *accidentally* said the wrong thing. Connor was certainly capable of such a mistake.

But then, Ashley glanced down at her soulmark, the letters so clear against her skin as they spelled out 'Connor'.

Somehow that seemed to add fuel to Ashley's anger. She slammed her car door before heading inside the building.

As she'd expected, Ashley found Connor in the kitchen. He turned to smile at her, but Ashley was on a mission. She had no time for smiles and certainly no time to appreciate how Connor was making them blueberry pancakes.

"I went to see Scott this morning, ask him for advice about what might've gone wrong with this job in Dallas," Ashley told Connor. She wanted to make absolutely sure that he knew why she going to ask him about it. "He said you wrote me a reference." Her tone was icily cold and Ashley could see Connor's body still.

"Are you the reason they don't want to employ me anymore, Connor?"

She almost didn't need to hear him answer. Connor was

not a very good liar - she could see guilt in the slight hunch of his shoulders, the way his eyes darted to either side of her face like he couldn't bear to look her straight in the eyes.

Still, Ashley waited, and she could see the dawning defeat in Connor's expression when he realized she was going to *make* him answer.

"I thought-" Connor began before he stopped. "I thought if you got another job, you wouldn't have to go so far away."

The answer really hurt.

Yes, Ashley had anticipated it. All the clues led to this. But she had *hoped* that maybe she'd misread it. Or even that maybe Connor didn't *know* he'd done something wrong. But the expression on his face, as much as his words... Connor knew. Not only did he know, but he had *intentionally* ruined Ashley's chances at something she had wanted to do.

It took her a moment to manage to speak again, the blood in her body running ice cold before just as quickly turning fiery hot. The anger flashed through her so *fast*. Ashley felt it was lucky she didn't have something to throw at a wall right that second.

"How fucking *dare you!*" She shouted, voice echoing around them. "This was *not* your decision to make!"

Connor's eyes widened. She could see something shift in him, the guilt falling away and his posture moving into something more defensive. "I want you to actually be *around*," he replied. He wasn't quite shouting, but his voice was nearly as loud as Ashley's had been. "You'd have been moving hours away, I'd never have seen you!"

The explanation - reason? - seemed to only add fuel to Ashley's anger. It wasn't *good enough*. "You *knew* how much this mattered to me! This was my chance to get my career started, to get on the right path," Ashley accused. The sheer arrogance of Connor presuming that he could choose for her, it angered her so much that briefly, Ashley struggled for more words.

The pause didn't last very long, though.

"And yesterday you *watched* me cry! You watched me

question what I did wrong when all along you knew it wasn't me. You weren't going to even tell me! You were just going to let me question my own fucking abilities when it's not *me*, it's *you*!" Ashley accused. "Is this some sort of a sick fucking game for you?"

It was one thing to lose her job, but it was a very different thing to know that *Connor* had made sure Ashley lost her job.

"Of course not!" Connor shot back. For whatever it was worth, he did look as though the idea shocked him. "You never wanted to think about what it would be like for me with you halfway across the country! You were so sure it would be *fine*, that we could just use the phone as if that would be enough."

"I never wanted to think about it? What, now you can read my mind?!" Ashley shouted. *Of course*, she thought about what it'd be like, how much she'd miss Connor and how much he might miss her. Staying optimistic had seemed a lot better than worrying about things she couldn't change. Except, of course, Connor had decided to change it for her.

Aside from everything else, Ashley found it so discouraging that Connor didn't even think they should bother *trying* a long-distance relationship. "If it hadn't worked, I would've considered coming back. I *know* that you can't just move with me, that you're tied into a contract. But you know what, Connor? At least I respect your career, which sure as shit is more than you clearly do for me."

Connor was pacing, looking like the kitchen was too small to contain him. He only stopped to pull the ruined pancakes off the heat. "That's not fair," he snapped. "I want you to have a job that you love. How was I supposed to know you'd have come back? You never said you would."

It was true, Ashley hadn't said so. What Connor didn't seem to take responsibility for was that he hadn't *asked*. There was no way Ashley could have known how much he was worrying because he'd seemed to understand what Ashley had worked towards. It was a chilling thought to realize that he never had.

"Do you? Do you want me to have a job that I love? Because to me, it seems like you just want me to be here for you! I'm not going to be your fucking trophy wife, Connor!" Even the thought of it *angered* Ashley. It wasn't until she'd voiced it out loud that Ashley realized how much that felt like what was happening. Like Connor was trying to *control* her life.

It took her a moment to compose herself, and then Ashley shook her head. "I'm not yours to keep, Connor. My career matters to me and I thought you understood that. I had a plan and I adjusted that plan to fit you in, but... that wasn't good enough for you."

That made him jerk his head up, his eyes flashing with irritation. "You adjusted it? What, by saying you could call and watch animal documentaries with me over FaceTime?" He scoffed, shaking his head. "That barely even *counts* as changing your plans." He was talking faster, the words tumbling from him as he tried to *defend* his decision, like he wasn't sorry, even now.

"I don't want you not to work, and I want you to do something you like, but if seeing me one weekend every couple of months is enough for you, then -" He stopped, catching himself, but Ashley could guess what he'd been going to say.

"Then what?" She pushed anyway. As far as Ashley could tell, Connor felt like what he'd done was *okay* and it definitely wasn't. She'd been so willing to give this a go, trusted that Connor *understood* her. Yeah, being apart would've been hard, but Ashley had honestly thought they could do it. It hurt to think that Connor hadn't, and rather than *talking* to her, he'd decided he could take her choices away from her.

Shaking her head, Ashley waved a hand at Connor. "You know what? Don't bother answering that. I can tell that you *still* don't think you've done anything wrong. That this was something you could choose for me. But you know what, Connor? *Fuck you.*"

There was nothing else to it. He was selfish and he was egoistic. *Ashley* didn't matter. Connor had made that pretty clear in both his actions and his absolute lack of regret. She just didn't have room in her life for someone who could care so little for her.

"Just leave," she said, shaking her head.

"What?" Connor sounded so dumb-founded, like he'd really believed that this was just a fight, something they could get over. It almost made him seem like he really *was* as stupid as Ashley knew he feared people thought him.

"I didn't mean to choose for you," he continued, with an edge of nervous tension in his voice now that hadn't been there before. "I thought there would be other jobs, and if you made one plan, you could make another one that would be just as good. Better, even."

"But you did decide for me. You could've talked to me, but instead, you went behind my back and told a job I worked so hard to get *not to hire me.*" And what stung about that, alongside everything else, was that Ashley *knew* Connor must've told them she was bad at it. Bad at doing PR when ironically that was the reason they'd gone into this whole thing in the first place.

Ashley couldn't help but wonder if this was at least partially her fault. If she had asked Connor how he really felt, or if she had just decided to stay in Madison, but Ashley also knew that it *wasn't* her fault. She couldn't let herself take the blame when it was Connor's to carry. *That* would be even more unfair.

"I thought you understood it. Understood me. I thought you got how much this job meant to me. But you don't. You only care about you and... I don't want to always come second to *you*, Connor. Coming second to hockey, I get. That's part of who you are. Coming second to you, though? That's unfair."

Ashley deserved more, she deserved *better*. And soulmate or not, Connor wasn't the right person for her if he didn't see that.

"Of course I care about you!" Connor insisted hotly. "That's *why* I didn't want you to move away, because you -" He stopped, catching himself and starting again. "Because we make *each other* happy." He didn't sound as sure as Ashley knew he would've done a week ago. Maybe he was right to doubt it. They certainly weren't making each other happy right now.

"If you stay, we can be together," he said. "Not just once or twice a month. We can have a real relationship, figure out if we are soulmates."

If she stayed.

But Connor had gotten rid of Ashley's option to leave, hadn't he? Sure, she could move home, but that was about it. Moving without having a job might be a luxury someone playing NHL hockey might afford, but it certainly wasn't one a normal person could afford.

Ashley had also felt that this was a real relationship, that like adults they could try to make things work before deciding that they didn't. The whole thing was making her question whether she even *knew* Connor.

"We can't have a real relationship. A real relationship means talking to each other, making sure we look out for each other. It doesn't mean going behind the other person's back and ruining something they worked really hard for." Ashley just felt so *defeated* by this.

It kind of hurt that all she'd done was prove herself right - soulmates weren't a *good* thing - if Connor even was her soulmate.

"Just go," she said, shaking her head and waving her hand towards the door. "I want you to go and I don't want you to come back." This wasn't going to work, and it felt *too* real at this point.

When Connor tried to speak again, Ashley shook her head. "No," she stopped him. "I just want you to leave, Connor. I don't want to see you again." And yeah, that *hurt* to say, but right now Ashley couldn't imagine a time she wouldn't be *angry* and so fucking *devastated* by what he'd done.

It took Connor a moment. When he finally did leave, the door softly closing behind him, Ashley sat down where she'd been standing.

As the tears came, all Ashley could think of was how it really, really sucked when your soulmate broke your heart.

CHAPTER ELEVEN

Connor

The door of Connor's car slammed closed. For good measure, he thumped his fist hard against the steering wheel. He was so *angry* with Ashley. The things she'd accused him of were so *unfair*. Connor knew that he cared about her, more than he'd ever cared for any of his other girlfriends. For Ashley to just dismiss that and send him away *hurt* so badly that the anger was easier for Connor to focus on.

He'd realized, when Ashley had cried to him about losing the job, that it had been more important to her than he'd thought. By then it had been too late. Connor had tried to convince her - and himself - that there would be other jobs, jobs that were just as good. He still half-believed it. Ashley hadn't even been willing to *look*.

Part of him wanted to storm back up to Ashley's door and demand she let him in so they could talk. Her words were still ringing in Connor's ears. Ashley didn't want him to come back, she didn't want to see him again. Connor couldn't process it. She'd calm down, he told himself, and then they could talk *reasonably*.

Except, if Ashley did calm down, Connor didn't get any

word of it. It was Scott who sat him down the next day, talked through with Connor what he wanted to tell the press.

If it had been up to Connor, he wouldn't have told them anything. He tried to get Scott to put it off, explaining that he and Ashley would fix things. What he hadn't accounted for was that Ashley had called Scott first, and made it clear there was no way she intended to carry on with their soulmate charade, let alone their actual relationship.

Connor had to deal with the pitying pats on the back from the Howlers, and the reports from Tex of Ashleys who'd tried to sneak past him into the rink to offer Connor comfort in his time of need.

It wasn't *their* comfort Connor wanted. Every time he changed the sticker covering his soulmark, he felt sick to his stomach.

It was weeks before Connor admitted to himself that Ashley wasn't going to answer any of his messages. She'd meant it when she said she didn't want to see him again. For the first time in Connor's life, hockey didn't make him feel better. The bitterest pill to swallow was that the Howlers were doing so well, making it through to the play-offs on a record streak of wins. Without Ashley there to kiss him for good luck, none of it seemed to *matter*.

"Lewis!" Coach stopped Connor on his way out after morning training. "Hang on a second, Hayden wants a word."

Connor headed back into the locker room, shoulders slumped as he sat on the bench and waited for everyone else to leave. Hayden sat opposite him. He was silent for so long that Connor finally looked up.

"I'm not going to pretend I know what you're going through," Hayden opened, "but you've been distracted for nearly a month. I thought -" He shrugged one shoulder, trailing off. "I think you need a person to talk to, and if you don't want it to be me, that's fine, but I want you to promise me that you'll find *someone*."

"What is there to say?" Connor asked, feeling the same

mix of hopelessness and irritation that had been his constant companion since he'd last seen Ashley. "She doesn't want to see me anymore, Hayden." Hayden hummed, just loud enough for Connor to hear, his gaze somewhere to the left of Connor's ear.

"What happened?" he asked. "You know how gossip gets around this place, but no one seems to know. One day you were happy, and then next -" He waved a hand, to indicate Connor's current state.

Even the idea of explaining it was painful. Connor seriously considered walking out or lying. He hadn't told anyone, not even his mom. *Definitely* not Maisy, who'd have a few well-chosen words about how much of an idiot Connor was.

"We had a fight," Connor said, through gritted teeth. "I don't know how to fix it. She said I wanted a trophy wife, and that I didn't care about her. You know that's not true!" He hated how whiny his voice sounded.

"I do," Hayden agreed. The wash of relief that Connor felt was short-lived. "I don't know Ashley well, but I'd bet she had good reasons for saying those things." When Connor didn't answer, didn't *object*, Hayden nodded. "Have you tried to fix it?" he asked.

"I've sent her a million messages!" Connor answered. "She won't answer me. I don't even know if she's reading them." Connor didn't know whether to hope she was or hope she wasn't.

"What have they said?" Hayden asked, making Connor's head jerk up. "Not the details," he quickly clarified, "just in general. Have you said you're sorry for your part of the fight?"

Connor wanted to object that there hadn't *been* a part of the fight that was his. It wasn't true. He'd gone behind Ashley's back. He'd *thought* he had good reasons, but Ashley was right that Connor could have talked to her. He still didn't believe that Ashley would have changed her plans for him, but he hadn't really given her the chance.

"I haven't," Connor admitted. "I don't see what good it would do. She doesn't want my apologies, and she doesn't want me around." Connor knew he sounded sulky, but he couldn't help it. He *missed* Ashley so much. It clouded every other feeling, and all people could tell him was that he'd get over it. "What if she was my soulmate, and I never feel any better?" he asked.

Hayden looked thoughtful. Connor found himself actually curious about what Hayden's take on that would be. It wasn't something Connor had let himself bring up to anyone else.

"If you still think she might be your soulmate, don't you think you owe it to yourself to apologize?" Hayden asked. "To do whatever you can to make things a little less painful between you?"

Connor frowned, puzzled by Hayden's wording. "You don't think she'll take me back, just because I say sorry," he noted. It didn't *sound* like Hayden was saying that he thought an apology was the way to get Ashley back.

"I don't know," Hayden answered. "Only she can *know*, and you've got a better idea of whatever you both said and did than I have. I just think if it were *my* soulmate, even if I didn't think I could get them back, I'd want to do whatever I could to… help them move on, I guess. Isn't that what a soulmate *means*? That you love someone else more than you love yourself?"

Connor had never thought of it that way. He hadn't even let himself think about whether he *loved* Ashley. It was too painful. What use was loving someone who didn't want to speak to you?

"It seems to me that it might do you *both* some good if you could clear the air," Hayden continued. "It might not mean you ever get back together, maybe that ship has sailed. Wouldn't you feel better if you weren't still carrying around unresolved anger towards each other?" That made Connor raise an eyebrow, and Hayden chuckled.

"I just mean," he explained, "that you might feel calmer if you knew you'd done everything that you could." Hayden stood up, offering Connor a hand. "You don't have to do anything right now. Just think about it. Or speak to someone else, if you think

I'm talking nonsense."

Connor *didn't* think Hayden was talking nonsense. Not entirely. He didn't think an apology would make Ashley forgive him, but maybe Hayden had a point that there were other goals beyond getting Ashley to take him back.

Sitting on his couch, with some incomprehensible physics documentary playing in the background, Connor scrolled through his unanswered messages to Ashley. He hadn't apologized. He hadn't even admitted that he'd been wrong, because that would be as good as saying that Ashley *should* have gone to Dallas. That was a thought too uncomfortable to face.

Now, Connor couldn't help thinking about what Hayden had said. If he really loved Ashley, if he thought she was his soulmate, then shouldn't he want her to be happy? Connor had gotten so tangled up in how he'd miss her. He'd forgotten that Ashley *wanted* to move. Not away from him, but towards her own future, just like Connor had moved away from people he'd loved to play hockey.

She was right. It had been selfish to try to stop her. He should have supported her. Connor could have helped her come up with ways the two of them could manage the distance, rather than just being disappointed by what had felt like inadequate efforts on her part. As she'd said, a real relationship included looking out for each other. Connor had spectacularly failed to do that.

It was *probably* too late to fix it now. It had been weeks, and the job had surely been filled. Connor knew from the reply to his email spoiling Ashley's job prospects that the hiring manager was a huge hockey fan, so maybe there was a *chance*.

Nearly a week later, Connor stood outside Ashley's door, feeling sick with nerves. He *ached* to see her. At the same time, he couldn't imagine how much it was going to hurt to see her and not be able to touch her, not to mention dealing with whatever her feelings were towards him.

He'd been stood there for nearly half an hour, waiting for Ashley to come home. At least, he *hoped* that she was out, rather than just ignoring him. He almost convinced himself to knock again, when suddenly she was there. Before he could see her expression go hard and angry, Connor launched into an explanation.

"I'm not here to bother you," he said. "I get it. You don't have to forgive me just because I want you to. If you say you don't want to see me again, I'll go." He paused for half a breath, just on the off chance that Ashley would jump in, say she *did* want to see him and everything would be okay.

She didn't.

"You can still have the job in Dallas," Connor forced himself to say. Some stupid part of him hated the thought of Ashley going, even now. If she was across the country, there'd be *no* chance that she might one day decide to take him back. Connor pushed that part down deep. "I called the hiring manager, and I explained -" Well, it didn't matter exactly *what* Connor had explained, so he waved a hand.

"The job's yours if you want it. The same start date, the same salary, everything." Connor had been very insistent on that point. "That's all I wanted to tell you." It wasn't really *all*. Connor had planned to leave as soon as he'd said his piece, but found himself unable to walk away.

"I'm sorry," he said, his voice low. "I'm sorry I ever tried to stop you from taking it. You were right, I was being selfish and short-sighted. All I could think about was how much I'd miss you. I thought that if you'd miss me too, then maybe you'd be happier if you could stay nearby. It wasn't my decision to make." Connor risked a glance into Ashley's eyes. His biggest worry was that she'd still be so angry that she wouldn't take this if it was *him* that was offering it to her. "You should take it," he urged. "You should go, and do all the things you planned to do." And this time, she wouldn't leave behind a boyfriend or a potential soulmate to worry about.

Ashley stopped, presumably waiting to see if Connor was done before she gave a nod. Connor had no idea what the nod *meant.* She wasn't asking him to *leave*, so he decided that was probably a good start. Walking past Connor, towards the door, she unlocked it before stepping inside.

"Come on, I don't need my neighbors to hear this." Connor followed her inside before she could change her mind. He wondered if he should apologize *again*, but then would that just seem like overkill? He had no idea. This wasn't something Connor had known how to prepare for and Ashley was so *silent* that it was very difficult to tell what she was thinking.

Setting her shopping bags down on the kitchen counter, Ashley turned around. It struck Connor how it was a very similar position they'd been in the last time he was there, just with him in the middle of the kitchen and her at the door.

"That's quite a speech, did you practice it?"

"No," Connor answered, and then paused, realizing that at this point he really had nothing to lose. "The first bit I did," he admitted, "about the job, that it was exactly the same as it was before. I didn't want you *not* to take it because it was me that was offering it." Connor still hoped that Ashley wouldn't refuse it on those grounds. She *deserved* to have the dream job that she'd worked so hard for.

"I was going to just leave, after that, so that you wouldn't have to deal with me." Maybe Connor should have, but Ashley had let him in, and she wasn't shouting at him. At least, not yet. "I *am* sorry," he added, "but I know that doesn't really change anything. I still did it. Even if I do my best to fix it, and even if I apologize. You won't be able to trust me again."

Ashley paused and Connor could appreciate that she gave him the time to speak. She seemed to actually listen, too. "Do you think what you did was wrong?" Ashley asked, glancing away from Connor. Before he had a chance to reply, she carried on talking.

"You really hurt me. It felt like you don't think my dreams and career ambitions are anything worth considering."

Connor winced. It felt a little like Ashley was twisting a knife *already* painfully piercing his heart, but he squared his shoulders. He deserved it. Whatever Ashley might have to say to him, it couldn't hurt worse than knowing he'd lost her.

"Yes," he answered simply. "It was wrong, and it was selfish, but I never *meant* to make you feel your career wasn't worth considering. I just thought…" Connor shrugged and sighed. Maybe there was no point defending himself, but Ashley *had* asked. "I thought there'd be other jobs that were just as good, that if something happened to make you reassess, you'd realize that you'd be happier." That was *mostly* true. "I suppose I convinced myself," Connor admitted, "because I *wanted* to believe you could be happier if you stayed."

"I wish you had just talked to me," Ashley said. She sounded so *honest* that it was almost painful. Connor, too, in retrospect wished he'd just talked to her. It was obvious that he'd been so focused on one thing he'd completely failed to think of an alternative. Putting some of her shopping into cupboards, Ashley turned back to look at Connor.

"Would it really have been so terrible to *try* long-distance?" Her tone sounded so defeated, that it was hard not to step forward to hug her.

Not wanting to make it worse, Connor paused, really thinking about his answer. "I don't know," he finally admitted. "You seemed so sure that it would work, and I couldn't really see it." Even *if* they'd talked about it, Connor didn't know that they would've come to an agreement on that.

"I guess I should have tried it before deciding. Or at least talked to you about what we were going to do if you got promoted in Dallas and wanted to stay there for years." Connor had never *had* a long-distance romantic relationship. Maybe it wouldn't have been as bad as he imagined.

"Yeah," Ashley nodded. 'Talking about it' seemed like the correct plan of action, if Connor had taken it. It was frustrating because it seemed like such a *simple* plan and yet Connor hadn't even truly considered it. Because of that, he'd lost Ashley. Worse still, he had *hurt* Ashley.

The silence stretched between them. Connor wondered if he should just *go*. Maybe Ashley would prefer him to go because his being there was just a reminder of how he'd failed her. For Connor, he couldn't help thinking about how *good* Ashley had been as a girlfriend. It made it hurt so much worse to think about her moving away, and the possibility that Connor would never see her again.

"I hope you will take the job," he said, his voice quiet. "I know it's none of my business, anymore, but I want you to be happy." The way Ashley looked up as if she were *surprised*, made Connor's heart ache. He wanted to explain, to make her understand.

"I know it doesn't seem like that was important to me," he said. "I'm sorry for making you feel like your happiness was less important than mine. I should have supported you. That's what you deserved. If I could go back-" If he could go back, Connor would do *everything* differently. "I'd make sure you knew that your happiness was most important."

"Was it, though?" Ashley asked, the challenge in her tone clear. "If it was so important to you that I be happy, why couldn't you respect that I *wanted* this job? Can you imagine what it would feel like if I took away your opportunity to play for the Howlers?"

Connor took a step back, bracing himself against Ashley's kitchen counter. He'd never been very good at being put on the spot. All he could think to do was tell Ashley the truth.

"I can't imagine," he said, shaking his head. "And I know you'd never do that." Ashley had always been understanding of Connor's commitments. She'd *never* made him feel bad for not putting her ahead of hockey. It was like she'd said, she'd been willing to come second to his passion for his sport. It was far more than Connor had deserved.

Connor didn't really *have* an answer for why, but Ashley seemed perfectly willing to wait in silence until he could come up with one.

"I thought I could make you happy," he said. "That us being together would make you happy, I mean. And I didn't realize that *this* job was so important, or that you'd gone through so much to get it."

Realizing those were just excuses, Connor ran a hand through his hair. "I *didn't* respect what you wanted, and you were right to break-up with me because of it."

The nod Ashley gave in confirmation *hurt* but it was deserved. Connor had breached her boundaries in a way that he *now* saw as unacceptable. No amount of good intentions would fix that.

"You did make me happy," Ashley said drawing Connor's attention back to her from where he'd been looking down, in some expression of shame. "But I don't want my happiness to depend on one person. As much as I wanted to be with you, I also wanted to be more than just someone's girlfriend, or someone's soulmate."

Connor nodded. As much as he hadn't acted like it, he did understand that. "I like that you're passionate about what you do," he said, and the force of Ashley's incredulous look almost made him take a step back.

"I know," he assured. "I wish I could have behaved as if I did when it mattered." It was no use starting *now*. Maybe the truth might clear the air, as Hayden had suggested. "I never wanted to put you in a position where you'd have to give it up and *just* be my girlfriend. If I'd known how much that particular job meant to you, rather than convincing myself that any PR job would be as good, -" Connor stopped.

"I should have known," he corrected. "You'd have known if it were the other way around. Or you'd have asked. You wouldn't have convinced yourself that the world would work out the way you wanted. You deserve better treatment."

"I do," Ashley nodded and Connor assumed this was where she told him to leave. When that didn't come, he gave her a small glance. Ashley seemed to be thinking about something and when she finally spoke up again, it surprised Connor.

"What you did was shitty, and inconsiderate, and hurtful," she listed and each word felt like being checked into the boards. He deserved it. "But," and that was not something Connor had expected so he looked up, not sure if he'd heard Ashley right. "I miss you. Miss the way you'll just sit on the sofa with me, I miss how you'll tell me about hockey even though you know I know nothing about it. I miss your attentive listening even when I know you don't know what it is I'm talking about. I miss how you smell and I miss how you *feel*. I really fucking miss you, Connor, and I really fucking hate that you made this so hard for us both."

Ashley's words seemed to break something in Connor's chest. He wasn't sure if it was his heart or the first crack of the walls he'd tried to build around himself, letting some hope through after weeks of despair. "I miss you too," he said, sincerely. "Everything about you."

That wasn't what was most important, though, because missing Ashley was Connor's own fault. "I hate that I hurt you," he agreed. "I know I deserve to miss you, but you didn't do anything to deserve feeling like I didn't value you. I know giving you the choice to take the job doesn't fix that, but I wanted to do *something*, fix whatever part of it I *could* fix."

Connor shook his head, having to make a conscious effort not to close the distance between them. "If there were anything I could do to not have hurt you, I would. Even if it were to leave the Howlers."

"Don't be stupid," Ashley said shaking her head, an instant response to Connor's proclamation. "It'd make you miserable, I would never want that." Not that leaving the Howlers would *achieve* anything anyway. It wouldn't magically fix this, but Connor really *would* do anything to take away the hurt he'd left behind.

He watched Ashley tap her fingers against the kitchen counter. She seemed to be thinking about something. Not for the first time he wished he could just read her mind. This would all be so much easier if Connor could read her mind.

"Would you want to try again?" She asked looking up at Connor. "Even if I did move to Dallas?"

Connor's heart gave a lurch because he hadn't thought it was *possible* for them to try again. It did also ache in his chest at the thought of Ashley moving. Now that he knew what it was like to have *no* Ashley, he knew that even seeing her infrequently would be better than not seeing her at all.

Still, Connor paused. Not because he had any hesitation, but because he wanted to show Ashley that he *was* thinking it through. He wasn't rushing into this as blindly as he'd rushed into hurting her. "I would," he finally said. "I'd miss you, and it would be hard, but knowing you were doing what made you happy would make it easier."

He ran his tongue over suddenly dry lips and did take a half-step forward. "Is that something you'd consider?" he asked, trying not to let hope overpower him, and failing spectacularly. Ashley could break his heart now. She could tell him she'd never take him back. Connor trusted that she wouldn't be spiteful enough to hurt him that way *deliberately.*

The pause felt like *forever.* Connor was willing to wait if it meant that on the other end of it he might be with Ashley. He'd never wanted anything so much in his whole life, except maybe to play hockey for the NHL. Connor knew how good *that* felt. To imagine that he could have two things in his life that felt that good, it was almost overwhelming.

"I can't just forget what you did, how much it hurt me," Ashley said. "But I do believe that you're sorry. I don't want to hold a grudge for the rest of my life. Yeah, it was shitty of you. It was possessive in a way that really frightened me, but I don't think you meant it possessively."

"I didn't," Connor confirmed quickly. "I can see how it

seemed that way. It doesn't make it any *less* shitty, but I really didn't mean it to be controlling." Connor's reasons had been bad. In hindsight that was obvious, but he'd never intended - or wanted - to control Ashley's life choices.

"No," she agreed, and Connor was almost surprised by how much relief he found in that agreement. Ashley *knew* him well enough to know that while his decisions had been shitty, they hadn't been anything more than shitty with good intention. "Will you promise to always talk things through with me? To never go behind my back even when you think it's for the best?"

Connor didn't have to hesitate over that, at all. "I promise," he said, taking another half-step. He wanted to pull Ashley into his arms and kiss her, pour all his regret and hope and longing into physical action, but he held back. "I'll talk to you, even when I think I'm not going to like what you have to say. I'll actually listen, and try to put myself in your shoes."

It was a lot to promise. Connor knew all he'd have to do was remind himself what it had been like to lose Ashley completely, and then *any* conversation, no matter how hard, would seem like the better option.

When Ashley didn't say anything straight away, Connor wondered if he needed to make even more promises. He could, and he would have, gladly. Then Ashley gave a nod. Connor's heart leaped in hope. "Alright." Before Connor could ask what that *meant*, Ashley had crossed the kitchen, her lips against Connor's. The kiss wasn't soft, but then Connor didn't *care*, his hands instantly coming to wrap around Ashley and pull her in closer.

She felt so perfect in his arms. For an instant, Connor wondered if this was all a dream he was going to wake up from, until Ashley bit down lightly on his lower lip, making Connor moan. She took advantage of his open mouth, sliding her tongue in. This was really happening.

Connor lifted Ashley almost off her feet, one hand at the small of her back and the other sliding into her hair. It was every bit as hot and intense as the first time they'd kissed, only *more*.

Connor pushed Ashley back toward the kitchen wall, lining his body up against hers.

There was a small sound that Ashley gave against his lips when her back hit the wall. She then brought a hand up to tug Connor in closer by his hair, so he took it to be a *good* sound. Ashley's other hand was pulling Connor's shirt up and she wrapped her legs around his waist, with Connor's hand supporting Ashley's weight. He pulled back only briefly enough to let her pull his shirt off, Connor's hand sliding under Ashley's shirt.

Ashley gave another moan in the kiss, hips rocking against Connor's already half-hard cock. He pulled back to give her jaw a small bite. Leaving a trail of kisses against Ashley's neck, he enjoyed the way her breath hitched in response.

"Fuck," Ashley breathed. "I really fucking missed you touching me."

Connor almost *growled* in response, the sound rumbling through his throat. "Want to do more than just touch you," he assured her, before kissing her again. The longer it went on, the more Connor *wanted*. Judging by the noises Ashley made, and the way her nails scraped against his back, she fully agreed.

"Come on," Connor urged, forcing himself to pull back. If they didn't go to the bedroom *soon*, he was going to end up getting Ashley naked in her kitchen. Connor would prefer not to make love in the room where they'd so recently argued. "Shall I carry you to the bedroom again?" he asked, remembering how Ashley had appreciated it the last time.

She only had to nod, and then Connor had lifted Ashley up in his arms, cradling her against his chest as he carried her through to gently drop her on Ashley's bed.

CHAPTER TWELVE

Ashley

Ashley really, really had missed Connor. At first, she'd told herself that she shouldn't. Then she'd felt guilty for missing him, but it hadn't negated the fact that she really had. There wasn't an excuse for what Connor had done and Ashley didn't want to excuse him. It had been shitty and it had hurt her a lot. That had added to Ashley's guilt for missing him.

What had helped a lot was talking to her mom. Ashley had gone over everything that had happened, starting with the fake soulmates thing and finishing with how she thought that there was a chance that Connor *was* her soulmate.

At first, Ashley had been somewhat worried about what her mom might say. Holly Walton had married someone who didn't have the name of her soulmark, she'd raised Ashley with the knowledge that a soulmark didn't have to define who you ended up with. It seemed a little bit like she was going to let her mom down by telling her that actually, Ashley thought she might be in love with the man who *did* carry the same name as her soulmark.

Holly hadn't disapproved. Instead, she'd listened patiently and then reminded Ashley that men - whether ones who were your soulmark matches or ones who weren't - in general, were pretty fucking stupid. It had startled a laugh from Ashley. From there on, she'd begun putting what had happened behind her.

Then Connor showed up, telling her how he'd gotten her job in Dallas back for her. He'd apologized and truly sounded like he recognized why what he'd done was wrong. Ashley wanted to get past it. She couldn't *forgive* him but that wasn't really necessary. Ashley could still think that what Connor had done was shitty but also try to have them *both* move past it.

His genuine regret made Ashley willing to *try*.

"Fuck," Ashley's breath caught when Conner dropped her down on her bed, bouncing them both. She slowed down then, brushing her hand over Connor's bare side. His skin felt hot and Ashley suddenly felt so overcome with emotion. She'd missed this, missed *him*. Having her fingers now free to roam Connor's body, it felt like he was coming home to her. Or maybe like she was coming home to him. Connor seemed to notice her hesitation. He paused to make sure she was okay.

That just made Ashley want him *more*. With one hand against Connor's side, Ashley brought her other to brush over his cheek. "It feels good, to have you so close again," she told him gently. Her hand was caressing over Connor's skin, fingers every so often sliding over his waistband. She wanted to show him how much she missed him. Wanted him to show her how much he'd missed *her*.

Connor settled his weight to one side of her, holding himself up so he wouldn't pin Ashley to the mattress. He pressed a kiss to her jaw. His warm breath against Ashley's ear, sent shudders down her spine. When he kissed her again, sucking her earlobe between his lips and teasing it with his tongue, Ashley felt like her whole body might melt.

"I want to make you feel good," Connor said, his voice a low rumble. He ran his fingers slowly down Ashley's side, skimming over the material of her top. He seemed in no hurry, lifting it only enough for him to expose a strip of bare skin over the waistband of Ashley's jeans. His hand was warm as it settled against her hip, thumb rubbing teasingly against her stomach. "I missed all of you," he promised. "Not just this."

The words made Ashley's body heat up more. She enjoyed how *slow* Connor was. It felt like he wanted to drink her in, take his time. She liked the idea that they could, that there was plenty of time to take. Ashley's hands brushed over Connor's shoulders as she tilted her head back so he could kiss her. His lips were soft. Ashley took her time to savor the taste, her tongue running over Connor's lower lip almost exploratorily.

This felt *different*. It felt *more*. There was a need between them. Ashley wondered if it was brought on by longing, because she *had* longed for Connor. Now having him here, between her legs, with her pressed against the bed, it felt right.

"I missed all of you, too," Ashley murmured truthfully. "Not just this," she added before giving Connor a grin. "But also definitely this." She loved having his body pressed up against hers. She could trace her fingers over every muscle. She wanted to feel *more* of Connor. "Help me take my shirt off?"

He kissed her while his hands moved slowly over her skin, like he was relearning the shape of her body. He only pulled away when he *had* to, helping her tug the material over her head. Kissing her again, he ran fingers through her hair before he shifted to straddle her. His mouth was so *hot* as it moved down Ashley's body, pressing kisses to her throat and her shoulder. "Definitely this," he agreed, as his hands swept up to cup Ashley's breasts through the lace of her bra.

He teased her nipples until they were hard against the fabric, then brushed his thumbs over both of them at once. It almost took Ashley's breath away. Pleasure sparked from everywhere Connor touched her. He pulled back, gaze moving over Ashley's body while he sucked his lower lip between his teeth. "You're so beautiful," he said, leaning in once again to kiss the upper curve of Ashley's breast.

She knew he meant it, too. The way Connor's eyes seemed

to roam her body like he truly *admired* it, it made Ashley feel beautiful. "You're not too bad either," she told him, the tone teasing. Connor was a great deal more than just 'not too bad' and Ashley knew he knew it. Her hands stroked over his beautiful arms, so strong and muscled. Then to his back, equally stunning. Ashley's hands ran lower until she gave a playful squeeze to Connor's ass through his pants.

His lips then brushed over her nipple, through the material of the bra. Ashley's breath caught, the sensation shooting all the way through her. Connor's touch was gentle but definitely firm. His hands slid down to her hips, brushing over the material there, before running up again, exploring her stomach. His fingers were hot and Ashley liked just how much care he took to kiss her breasts.

"Want to help me out of the bra?" She asked, certain that they both would enjoy this even more if she was fully topless.

"I thought you'd never ask," Connor answered, with a playful smile. Almost immediately he sobered. Ashley knew, without needing to hear him say it, that Connor really *had* thought they'd never have this again. Ashley had thought so too. The relief that it wasn't the case washed over her. Connor seemed to feel the same, judging by the way he pulled her close to kiss her again. "I -" He stopped, lowering his head to nuzzle against the curve of Ashley's breast.

His strong fingers easily found and opened the clasp of her bra, and he pulled back to help Ashley free herself from it. When she met his eyes, he was smiling at her with such genuine affection. "I don't want to think about it right now," he said, his tone imploring. "Let's focus on this."

For a very short moment, Ashley wondered if they should talk. Then Connor pressed another kiss against her lips. No, they didn't have to. Not right now. They had plenty of *time*. Right now, Ashley wanted to do just as Connor had said and focus on this. Focus on them and how they were back together again. She pulled Connor in closer, her breasts pressing against his chest.

Without the material between them, Connor's skin felt

even hotter. Ashley's hands explored over it. She gave a soft moan when Connor flexed his arm muscles under her touch. Knowing how strong he was made Ashley's body tingle. Reaching for one of Connor's hands, she led it over her body. It felt as if she was reintroducing Connor to it. She knew he knew how to touch her just right, but Ashley wanted to show him how anyway.

She led his hand up to one of her breasts, moaning against Connor's lips when she pressed his hand against it.

His palm was so big. Ashley's breast fit into it almost perfectly. Connor shifted, his thumb flicking across her nipple. He swallowed Ashley's moan, his other hand settling against her waist as he pressed her down into the mattress. Kissing his way across her chest, Connor seemed to pay equal, undivided attention to every inch of Ashley's skin.

Finally, Connor moved down the bed. Not so far as to be out of Ashley's reach completely. She ran her hands over his shoulders and through his hair rather than all the way down his back. He circled his tongue around Ashley's nipple, making her arch up under his hands. When he blew warm air across her damp skin, Ashley couldn't hold back the little noises of satisfaction.

"You sound just as good as I remember," Connor rumbled, moving to give her other nipple the same treatment.

It was very *easy* to sound good for Connor when he teased like this. Ashley arched her back up, eager to have more of Connor's mouth against her. He obliged gladly, his tongue swirling around Ashley's nipple. It made her moan louder. Connor had to press a hand against Ashley's hip to hold her in place. It made Ashley feel good, like he didn't want her to leave. Not that she had any intention to.

Pulling on his arm, Ashley made Connor move back up so she could kiss him. Her tongue ran over his lower lip, lightly and teasingly. She followed it with a small bite. The way Connor's breath caught made her want to do it all over again.

"I'm on the pill," Ashley told him. It wasn't the most romantic of things to say, but it did allow her to then add, "I want to feel you inside me." And she really *did*. To have that, to have *him*.

Connor moaned, and the sound made Ashley realize how much she'd missed *that*, too. She loved knowing the effect she had on him. Even the *idea* of being inside her was enough to get a reaction. "I haven't been with anyone else," he said, the words almost rushing out of him. "I wouldn't have wanted to."

They'd been apart for a while. Ashley had no doubt Connor could have picked someone up. It was sweet that he hadn't, especially when he'd had no hope of their getting back together.

"I know," she said gently. Ashley wanted Connor to know that she believed him, that she trusted him, because she did. There was no doubt at all in her mind that he was truthful. It was, after all, one of the things they had agreed. Connor would talk to her and Ashley trusted that. She kissed him harder, more eagerly, pouring all that she could into that kiss.

Shifting under Connor, Ashley ran her hands down between them to undo the fastenings on Connor's pants. She could feel how hard he was. His cock pressed against her leg when he leaned in to kiss her and this time Ashley pushed back more, enjoying the cry Connor gave. She wanted more, wanted to make him give louder sounds.

Carefully, Ashley slid her hand under the material of Connor's pants. Her fingers brushed lightly over where his cock was pressing into his boxers. "I want you," she told him, tilting her head back more.

Connor took his cue from her, fitting his body against hers and pressing kisses to her exposed throat. She shivered. The feeling of his stubble scratching against her skin made her feel even more sensitive to the warmth of his mouth. "You've got me," he assured, pulling back only so that he could push his pants off.

He paused, smoothing his hands up Ashley's legs. "I want you to be wearing fewer clothes," he told her, grinning. It was good to see him playful and confident again. Ashley made no objections as he reached for the buttons on her jeans.

He didn't hurry over taking them off. Instead, he nipped at every exposed inch of Ashley's stomach, sliding the material away from her until only her panties remained.

Once upon a time Ashley might've felt exposed like this, but now she didn't. She trusted Connor so fully, knew that he wanted her as much as she wanted him. With him having pulled back, Ashley could drink in how truly beautiful and *sexy* he was. The curve of his shoulders, the smoothness of his stomach - she loved being able to just reach out and touch him. As a reward, Ashley saw a shiver run over Connor's skin. A shiver *her* touch put there.

"Kiss me again," she told him, smiling up at Connor. He didn't hesitate, his lips pressing against hers almost straight away. Moving her legs, Ashley let him slot between them, only the material of their underwear between them. She rocked her hips up, swallowing the moan that escaped Connor at the contact.

Heat built between them slowly as they rocked together, until Ashley felt sure they'd set each other on fire if they didn't *do* something. One of Connor's hands cupped her ass, lifting her hips so he could grind against her. "Fuck," he groaned, nipping at Ashley's lower lip before he licked into her mouth.

Connor didn't pull away from the kiss to undress her. Instead, he slipped his hand under the material of her panties. His fingers felt so *good* against Ashley's sensitive skin. It was hard to tell which of them moaned louder when he stroked gently through the wetness that had gathered.

It wasn't enough. Ashley wanted more, she wanted to *feel* Connor. Her hands pushed at his boxers, until he pulled his hand back so he could take them off. "And mine," she insisted lifting her hips. The way that made Connor laugh was very rewarding. Ashley *liked* that they could do this. That it didn't *have to* be all serious and sexy. It could be *fun* and sexy.

She lifted her hips more to help Connor remove her underwear once he'd disposed of his own. This time when he resettled on top of her, there was no material between them. Ashley could *feel* the heat rolling off of him.

"Show me? Show me how much you've missed me?" She asked, a soft moan falling from her lips even at the *thought*.

Connor pressed his body to hers, letting Ashley feel him *everywhere*. His hand moved between them, touching her so carefully as he made sure she was ready. "I did," he breathed, pressing his cock against her. "I missed you so much." He pushed forward, *filling* her. Ashley heard his breath catch in his throat.

He didn't stop until he was inside her completely, no space left between them. It was just what Ashley wanted. She tipped her head back as Connor's hips slowly rocked out and in once more. His thrusts were slow, but so *strong*, like he needed Ashley more than he needed air.

Ashley could feel the way her heart was beating against her chest. Or maybe it was the way Connor's heart was beating. He felt *perfect* against her and inside her. With a hand against the back of Connor's head, Ashley ran her fingers through his hair gently. "You feel great," she murmured before pulling him down for a kiss.

With Connor still moving slowly in and out of her, Ashley gave a string of soft moans, all of which were swallowed up by Connor's mouth. She wrapped her legs around Connor's waist as if to pull him in even closer. It encouraged Connor to start moving faster, sending thrills of pleasure through Ashley's body.

"Ah, yes, just like that," she moaned softly.

With their bodies so entwined, Connor's thrusts rocked Ashley against the bed. The two of them moved in harmony. As he increased the pace, Connor buried his face against Ashley's neck, crying out against her skin every time he pressed into her. She could feel his muscles flexing and releasing under her hands as she stroked over his back and ass.

"Ashley," he groaned softly, "you're *perfect*." One hand hitched Ashley's thigh even higher. The change of angle let him press deeper inside her. She could hear the noise he made as he tried not to buck his hips too hard.

Maybe under different circumstances, Ashley would've questioned how truly perfect she was. Or even pointed out that she *wasn't.* Right now, with Connor's body hard against her? Ashley was willing to just accept that. Especially when Connor's movement made her cry out in pleasure. A string of soft moans and chants of Connor's name fell from Ashley's lips.

This felt perfect, having Connor like this. Ashley moved faster under him, meeting every thrust as much as she could. The angle meant that Ashley's orgasm began building quickly and steadily. Before she knew it, the pleasure ran through her veins like fire.

"Oh God, Connor!" Ashley half-screamed, bucking up even more to urge him to go faster. He did, doing exactly what she wanted. The pleasure was immediate. A breathless scream got stuck in Ashley's throat as she came. Her fingers tightened against Connor's arm, probably leaving marks of *just* how strong an orgasm it had been.

She carried on moving, not wanting Connor to stop until he came, too. With her muscles tightening around him, it hardly took much more than a few thrusts. She felt him come, her name on his lips as he did so. Tilting her head back, Ashley sought out Connor's lips for a hard, passionate kiss.

They kissed until they were breathless. Ashley felt almost *giddy* from it. When Connor did pull away, it was with reluctance. He slipped free from her, but only far enough that his weight didn't pin her against the mattress. In his big hands, he scooped her body close against his side, one of his legs draped over both of hers.

He leaned in, kissing the angle of Ashley's jaw and the arch of her eyebrow. It almost seemed as though he was memorizing her face. Ashley recognized the feeling. In the weeks they'd been apart, she'd tried *not* to spend time remembering the exact blue of Connor's eyes, or the way his hair stuck up in a thousand directions.

Pressing a softer, sweeter kiss against her lips, Connor murmured, "I love you, Ashley."

The words made her smile, a warmth instantly settling in Ashley's stomach. She turned slightly in Connor's arms so she could bring a hand up to his cheek. Her fingers were soft as she stroked over it. Leaning in, Ashley brushed her nose against Connor's. There was something so intimate about how they were. Ashley didn't even a tiny bit doubt that Connor meant it. That Connor truly loved her.

"I love you, too," she told him gently. There was no hesitance in her voice. Ashley *knew* she loved Connor and it was easy to tell him as much.

"I'm a little afraid this will all be a dream, and I'll wake up just to miss you even more." There *was* a trace of anxiety in Connor's eyes as he said the words.

"I thought about you all the time," he said, "but I didn't think we'd ever be *here* again."

It was sweet. Ashley gave Connor a soft smile. She liked that he *told* her. It was a good indication that Connor was willing to truly try; to make this relationship better than it had been (and it had been good until it hadn't).

"It's real," Ashley promised, brushing her hand over Connor's arm. "I'm not going to take the job in Dallas," she said, turning so she'd have more space and a better angle to look at Connor. Her hand didn't leave his arm as it stroked over it.

"You - what?" Connor asked. Ashley had to bite her lip not to laugh at how obvious his surprise and confusion were. "But I thought it was your dream job? You had to do three different assessments and your Master's thesis just to have a chance at it?" It proved that he'd been listening, and Ashley found that reassuring, too. He bit his lip, gaze dropping and cheeks coloring slightly. "Is it because I ruined it?" he asked, and Ashley could tell that he genuinely thought it was a possibility.

"It's not about you," Ashley said, shaking her head. "Not really." Obviously, if Connor hadn't messed up her chances at the job in the first place - even if he had now fixed it - Ashley would've gone. She would've never even considered other options. So in a way, it *was* about Connor, but her decision to stay wasn't because of him, which was why Ashley found it easy to choose.

"Yes, if you hadn't... ruined it," she did consider using a different word, but frankly, that *was* appropriate. "I would've gone, but I've actually had a new job offer." There she paused before a small grin settled on her lips. "Scott offered me a job with the Howlers."

She watched as the emotions played out on Connor's face. She could *see* his hesitance to believe it before his mouth twitched into an irrepressible grin. He shifted even closer, warm hand spanning Ashley's back. "Really?" he asked, amazement obvious in his voice. "You're not teasing me?"

Ashley had barely started to shake her head before Connor was kissing her, shifting them around until Ashley was half on top of him. He pulled back, looking up at her. "That's *amazing!* Are you going to take it? Is it a good job?"

Those were fair questions. Pride swelled inside of Ashley when Connor asked them. She didn't doubt for a moment that if she said that it wasn't, or that she wasn't sure, he *would* support her decision. Besides, they had also been questions that Ashley had asked herself when Scott had offered. That and whether Scott was offering it to her *because* of Connor.

He had promised Ashley that Connor wasn't the reason. Scott was very impressed with how Ashley had handled Connor's PR. He wanted to train her to do the Howlers' PR on a greater scale. Ashley had to admit that as far as working for brands went, sports really hadn't ever featured in her plans. It was, however, a great opportunity and Ashley had *enjoyed* doing Connor's PR.

"It's a very good job," Ashley nodded. "I am going to take it." And if that meant that she got to be with Connor, well, that was just an added bonus.

Connor kissed her again as if it was easier to *show* her how pleased he was than put it into words. Ashley couldn't complain, not when Connor's tongue still felt *so good* as it teased against her own. Connor lifted a hand, running it through Ashley's hair and then pulling back, grinning his excitement up at her.

"They're not going to say we can't date if we work together, are they?" he asked. Unlike his earlier questions, this one sounded teasing. That was fair enough, given they'd started dating *because* they were working together.

Ashley dragged her hand up Connor's arm, fingers picking against the corner of the sticker hiding his soulmark before she pulled it off. "They can't stop soulmates from being together," she pointed out. And yes, maybe there was still a chance that they weren't, but there was just as much chance that they *were.* And for the first time in her life, Ashley felt *happy* at the idea that perhaps she did have a soulmate, and maybe she'd even met him.

"No one will stop us from dating," Ashley promised.

The smile Connor gave her at that was softer, and he ran his fingers over Ashley's soulmark, tracing the letters of his name. It took Ashley back to the first time she'd asked if he'd like to touch it. Such a lot had changed since then. Ashley really did think they were *both* happier now than they had been.

"My mom's going to be over the moon," Connor said, looking delighted at the prospect of telling her. "And Maisy's going to like you," he promised. "She'll probably side with you over everything, just to wind me up." He paused, eyes darting to Ashley's face. "Over trivial things," he corrected. "I know we might still have arguments, but I'll talk to *you* about them, not my sister."

Ashley laughed at that because it was just such a *genuine* thing to say and a very *Connor* thing to say. It was pleasing to think just how well she now knew him. "You can talk to us both," she teased, pressing another kiss against Connor's lips. "But I'll always be here to listen to you, yeah? Always."

Growing more serious again, Connor nodded. "I know you will," he confirmed, so sincerely. Ashley genuinely believed he meant it. It made her feel warm, knowing that Connor trusted her to be there for him. "And I'll do better at being here to listen to you," he promised in turn. "I don't ever want to hurt you again, and I know I probably *will*, accidentally, but I hope it won't ever be *so* bad."

His hand was still moving, almost reverently, over Ashley's soulmark. "I want to be the kind of soulmate you deserve," he said, "and I will learn how to be. No matter what." He gave her a grin, before adding, "I'm very good at doing things I set my mind to."

Ashley realized that she truly *believed* him. Her heart felt so heavy with love that she couldn't stop leaning in and kissing Connor. "We're going to make this work," she promised Connor, so sure of her words.

Licking her lips, Ashley grinned at Connor. "Your first task as a soulmate could feature using your mouth?" She offered, wiggling her eyebrows in a very comical display of suggestiveness. It made Connor laugh, just as Ashley had hoped it would. He did then lean in to press a trail of kisses against her neck.

She hardly needed more words when Connor's mouth and hands moved lower. His touch was soft and tender against her skin, sending shivers of heat through her. As she moaned Connor's name, Ashley was very sure this would work out for them.

Ashley's first month at the new job was *busy*. She honestly hadn't realized just how much work there was when it came to PR for an NHL hockey team. Not only was there the brand as a whole but also each individual player's PR. Some had their agents take care of it, but most relied on the Howlers' PR team. It was definitely a very steep learning curve. Ashley *loved it*.

Being so busy meant that Ashley didn't get as much time to spend with Connor. Then again, he didn't have much spare time either now that the Howlers were in the playoffs. Ashley didn't mind. In fact, she quite liked it. Having them both busy with work meant that they couldn't feel left out by the other. It helped that they both worked for the Howlers even if it was in *very* different roles.

Despite everything else, what Ashley liked the most was coming home to Connor or having him come home to her. Normally on game nights, Ashley was first to come home since Connor was out celebrating with the team. Tonight when she pulled up outside his house, the lights were on.

The house was warm and smelled *amazing*. After hanging her jacket up in the hall, Ashley made her way through to the kitchen.

"What's this?" She asked, finding Connor next to the stove stirring something in a pot. "I thought you'd be out with the team celebrating your win."

Connor smiled, leaving the spoon just long enough to press a kiss against Ashley's cheek. It was a casual gesture, almost as if Connor hadn't needed to think about it. Somehow, that made Ashley feel even more like she was *at home*, even if it wasn't *her* home.

"I went out for a drink," he told her, "but I wanted *us* to celebrate. We've been back together for exactly a month." He grinned, and Ashley knew that it made him genuinely happy.

"So," Connor carried on, gesturing with his free hand to the stove, "I'm making risotto, and there's a bottle of white in the fridge, *and* I've got a surprise for you." *That* was unexpected. Connor honestly wasn't very good at not telling people things, so if he'd planned a surprise, it must really have taken a concerted effort.

Ashley took a seat on one of the bar stools at Connor's kitchen island, smiling at Connor when he presented her with a glass of the said wine. "A surprise," she repeated. "Will I have to wait until after dinner for it?" If this was a *sex* surprise then she almost definitely would, but Ashley didn't think Connor would surprise her like that.

Connor hummed thoughtfully as he continued to stir the rice, then seemed to come to a decision. "No, I'll tell you the surprise before we eat, otherwise I'll end up telling you *during* dinner, and that'll ruin everything." He looked so eager, and so enthusiastic. It made Ashley very curious about what the surprise could be.

"It's not a present," he said as if reading Ashley's thoughts. Taking the pan off the heat, Connor stirred some butter into it, then put it aside. "Do you want to come to see it now?" he asked, picking up his own glass of wine.

"Yes, of course," Ashley nodded. For all that Connor wasn't very good at keeping a surprise secret, *she* was far too eager to find out what the surprise *was* to be truly patient. It was probably yet another way in which they were well matched.

Setting her glass down after another small sip, Ashley got up, ready to follow Connor to wherever this non-present surprise was. Walking over so she could tiptoe to kiss him, Ashley smiled against his lips.

"I like coming home to you," she said truthfully.

Now that his hands weren't busy with cooking, Connor wrapped one strong arm around Ashley's waist. He beamed down at her with a smile that made Ashley's heart seem to skip a beat. "I like having you come home to me," he echoed. "That's why -" He caught himself, pressing his lips firmly closed.

"Come on," he urged, taking Ashley's hand and leading her towards the bedroom. It was unusually tidy. Ashley considered asking whether *that* was the surprise, but before she could, Connor had put both hands on her shoulders and positioned her in front of the closet.

Stepping around her, he pulled the door open, like a magician unveiling a trick. Ashley didn't immediately *get it*. Connor must have noticed her lack of reaction because he waved a hand at the space where there were currently no clothes hanging.

"I moved my winter things out of the closet," he explained, "so that there'll be space for you to hang stuff."

"Oh," Ashley heard herself say. That was... she had no idea how she felt about that. *Good*, was the first thing that came to her mind. Connor had taken the time - God only knew *when* he'd had the time - to clean out a space for Ashley, to make sure she had a space in his home if she wanted it.

Somehow, Ashley had half-expected him to just ask her to move in with him. She would have said no, it was too soon. *That* just made her even more pleased. Connor must have expected that to be her answer and therefore *not* asked. Taking it slow wasn't his strong suit and yet he was trying for Ashley.

"I love it," she announced with a wide smile, turning to kiss Connor. "It's an excellent surprise." The way he smiled back was almost as great.

He wrapped his arm around her again, kissing her for a long moment before he pulled back. "That's why I'm so glad you like coming home to me," he explained, "because now you can leave some clothes here, and you can do it more often. Not *always*," he hastened to explain. "I know sometimes we'll go to your place, and sometimes you'll go to your place without me." He did give a little pout at that, but Ashley could tell it was teasing.

"I thought it would make things easier. And I like the idea of you hanging things in my closet. It feels... long-term." His eyes scanned Ashley's face, still smiling at her. "You really like it?"

"It's also more efficient," she teased. There were still times when Ashley worried that her planning of things, or the way she wanted things to be in a particular order, might be off-putting. But most days, she truly believed that Connor didn't mind. He did a lot to show her how not only he didn't mind but he *appreciated* the way she was.

And yeah, she really, really did like it. "I love it," she promised Connor. Giving Connor a wide smile, Ashley tiptoed to press another kiss against his lips. "I love you." She really, *really* did. "And I love that you want this to feel long-term."

"Such a lot of things you love," Connor teased, but he was beaming. It really made Ashley appreciate how easily it came to her to make Connor happy. "Maisy said I should buy you fancy scented coat-hangers," Connor told her dubiously, "but I *think* she was joking."

More seriously, he added, "I love you, so of course I want this to be long-term. You make everything better." He sounded so sincere, and he pulled Ashley close against his chest, like he still worried that he might lose her. "I *always* want you to be in my life," he said.

If possible, Ashley's smile widened even more. It was a fantastic realization to know that she *believed* him. Connor meant it, both that he loved her and that he wanted to always have her in his life. But more than that, Ashley knew he also wanted them both happy and was willing to work for that happiness.

Soulmates might still be something that Ashley didn't fully trust, but what she was very quickly learning was that being with Connor wasn't *about* having a soulmark that matched his. If they were soulmates, it was because they were good for each other. Sure, their names matched, but it didn't have to *define* them.

Getting over the fear that somehow Ashley was *obliged* to pick Connor was easy when she *wanted* to pick him. They'd make it work. They'd been a great fake couple, and they made an even better real couple.

Fake soulmates or not, Ashley didn't think it mattered.

Not for as long as they could be *happy*.

EPILOGUE

Connor

By the time the press conference had been going for nearly fifteen minutes, it had covered most of the actually hockey-related questions. After that, the reporters had to start getting creative.

"Connor, do you think your game has improved now that you have a soulmate?"

Giving a startled laugh, Connor paused to think. As much as he loved Ashley, and he did, he didn't think *she* would say that she'd improved his performance on the ice. He remembered what she'd said to him all those months ago about people wanting to believe that celebrities lived a charmed life. In many ways, Connor felt as if he *did*. It wasn't difficult to give an answer he thought people would like to hear.

"Everything about my life has improved now that I'm with Ashley," he said, and then grinned. "She doesn't give me tips on my game - I had to teach her the rules of hockey when we started dating." That got a laugh. Connor waited until it had quietened. "She makes me happier, and that means I sleep better, and I eat better, and I have less stress in my life. All of that makes a difference to my performance, in training and out of it."

Connor could see people nodding. He knew Ashley was nearby, listening. Connor didn't seek her out. He was better at handling the press now, thanks to Ashley's advice, but he always got distracted when she was in his line of sight. Sometimes he got impatient for the questions to be over so he could take her home.

"What's it like when you have to travel for away games? Do you mind having to leave your soulmate behind?"

Connor *did* mind, but there was no help for it. He and Ashley had talked about how it wouldn't really be good for anybody if she traveled with the team.

"I'm just glad we live in an age of technology," Connor joked. There was certainly truth to it, too. "I text her a lot, especially if we're on the road. And we make good use of FaceTime." His eyes briefly strayed, but he forced himself not to search for Ashley in the crowd. "It's not as good as being together in person, but it's a *lot* better than not talking to her at all."

It gave Connor a pang of regret, thinking about how he'd once dismissed phone calls and FaceTime as not good enough to keep their relationship alive. It always ached, to think of how much he'd hurt Ashley. The pain seemed to get weaker the further away from it they moved. In a way, Connor wouldn't want it to stop hurting completely, because he never wanted to make the same mistakes again. It was a reminder, and one that he valued, even if he didn't *enjoy* it.

"I miss her," he carried on, "but when I'm on the ice, it's easy just to focus on the game, on my teammates, and what we're there to do. I don't think anyone would say that I'm unfocused." He gave another grin. "She'd be the first to tell me off if I was. She's my best support, and of course she wants me to do well."

The questions moved on, and Connor let his attention wander as Nilssy answered questions about their strategy for the upcoming games.

Finally, he was allowed to leave the podium. He bounded past the gathered reporters to find Ashley.

"How did I do?" he asked, wrapping an arm around her waist and kissing her cheek. "Are you proud?"

Ashley's first response was a laugh, but she nodded soon after. "You did excellently," she promised, making Connor beam at her with satisfaction. "I doubt I'd be the first to tell you off. Maybe more like fifth." It was true that she'd have to get in line behind Coach, Nilssy and at least a few of the other guys on the team. It didn't really feel like a negative, though, to have so many people Connor could trust to be fair and honest with him.

After a moment's thought, he shook his head. "I still think you'd be first," he decided. "You'd *notice* first, even if you weren't there. You'd be able to tell that my head wasn't in the game. You'd say something to get me to concentrate." *If* Connor wasn't focusing on a game, it was true that the Howlers would get at him first. He honestly believed that Ashley would be able to tell long before it got to that point.

"You wouldn't really tell me off, though," he said. "At least, I don't think it would feel like telling off, not if I was distracted because I was missing you." Ashley was too sensitive for that and would find some *nicer* way of getting Connor to focus on hockey first.

"I wouldn't tell you off if you were missing me," Ashley agreed. "But I also have no plans to let you miss me." As the summer was quickly approaching, the two of them were making plans for how they could avoid missing each other. Or, well, mostly it was Ashley making plans. Connor just enjoyed that he didn't have to worry about anything. It was a pretty nice state of being.

"Your mom's been texting me about how excited she is that we're coming over," Ashley said almost as if she could read Connor's mind. (She couldn't, but sometimes he really did wonder).

He beamed. "I like that she texts *you* rather than me," he teased, putting on his best pout. He knew, without either of them having to say so, that both Ashley and his mom were making an effort to reach out to each other. It settled a warm glow in his stomach to know it was because of how much they cared about him.

"She texts me because I'm more reliable to actually arrange something," Ashley pointed out. Really, Connor couldn't object to that. Ashley was very good at planning things and Connor saw absolutely no reason to interfere.

"You're going to get on like a house on fire," Connor promised. He'd never got the sense Ashley was really *nervous* about meeting his mom, but she would hardly object to hearing, again, how confident Connor was that it would go well.

Ashley grinned. She clearly agreed because there was no attempt to suggest she *wouldn't*. "And then the week after we're going to visit my parents," she said a little teasingly. It would be the first time Connor would meet Ashley's mom and dad, too. He felt more nervous about that than Ashley did about meeting his mom.

"They'll like you," she promised. Again, Connor was sure she could just read his mind. "I can't read your mind, we've talked about this. It's just that your facial expressions give literally everything away," Ashley argued doing nothing for the cause.

"My dad's been learning hockey rules."

That made Connor give a startled laugh. "I think that makes me *more* nervous, not less," he playfully complained. His stomach filled with excited, if somewhat nervous, butterflies at the idea that Ashley's dad had gone out of his way to have something that they could talk about.

Connor *wanted* to meet them. Ashley had reassured him a number of times that they wouldn't think less of him for his soulmark matching Ashley's name, so he was mostly nervous about making a good impression.

"Did you tell him I can only talk about hockey?" he asked. Connor didn't think it was *true*. He did talk about hockey a lot, so maybe he wasn't a great judge.

"No," Ashley laughed. "I told him you can also talk to him about all the history documentaries he loves watching," she teased.

There were quite a few nights that Ashley and Connor had spent cuddled together on a couch watching documentaries. It was *nice* that this was something Connor could now share with someone. The idea that he might also be able to use it as a conversation topic with Ashley's dad was kind of amusing.

"I can try," Connor agreed, "as long as he doesn't mind reminding me of all the facts." Having talked over documentaries with Ashley, Connor felt less self-conscious than he once had about all the things he *didn't* remember. It helped to know there were things Ashley forgot, too.

It struck Connor as he led the way outside that he was looking forward to the summer a lot more than he usually did. He always loved visiting his mom, and Maisy, but he usually missed the intensity of training with the team, not to mention spending time with Blake and Nilssy and the rest of the Howlers.

"Are you sure you can handle a whole summer of me without half my attention being on hockey?" he asked Ashley. He was grinning as he said it.

"I don't know," Ashley answered. It was striking how *honest* she was. Like, yes, maybe she couldn't. "But I'm willing to try," she teased. That set all of Connor's nerves at ease. That was all they could ask from each other, to just try, and so far it was definitely working out well.

"We'll make it work," Connor said, repeating Ashley's own phrase back at her. He hadn't always been so sure. The better they got to know each other, and the more time they spent together, the more confident Connor was that they *would*.

That, Connor thought, was what it really meant to be a soulmate. He and Ashley didn't agree on everything, and their relationship hadn't all been easy and perfect. If it had been, it wouldn't have felt *real*. What they had, a willingness to work together, and overcome challenges, was worth so much more.

He linked his hand with Ashley's, his arm brushing against hers. Though his soulmark was covered by his sleeve,

Connor could imagine it reaching out invisibly to where he could just see his name against Ashley's skin.

They'd always make it work, not *just* because their soul-marks matched, but because they loved each other, which was a hundred times more important.

*Next in the Madison
Howlers series:*

Best Shot

Everyone in the world carries their soulmate's name written on their skin. Thea and Doe are best friends who would never fall out over a man. With Doe's soulmark reading 'Blake' and Thea's being 'Frederick', this has never been a problem they thought they might encounter.

Enter Blake Ashbury. Thea is the first to meet the gorgeous hockey player but as soon as she finds out he might be *Doe's* Blake, she takes her best shot at getting the two of them to hit it off. It doesn't matter that Thea's the one who loves Blake's jokes, or that his dimples make her want to keep causing his smiles forever. Doe and Blake are meant to be together, so Thea will back off. At least that's the plan.

Blake never expected meeting his soulmate to be so complicated. Doe is lovely. She's everything Blake thought he wanted in a girlfriend. He can't explain why he keeps getting drawn into conversations with Thea instead.

Thea and Blake aren't meant to be together, so *why* is it so hard to keep the chemistry between them down? The longer they spend together, the harder it becomes to remember that they need to keep their distance!

Printed in Great Britain
by Amazon